"Are you afraid of me, *dusci*?" Lorenzo all but purred. "I must admit, I cannot imagine why," he said with a silky arrogance that helped break through the haze affecting her.

"You can't?" she returned, finally finding her voice in her irritation with him. She forced herself to step outside, though she kept by the door. She would have an escape if she needed one. "When rumors swirl about you the way they do? None of them good?"

There was the tiniest flicker of something in his expression. Not violence, but that intensity she'd once been enthralled by. Still was.

"Tell me, Brianna. Do you believe every rumor you hear, or only ones about former lovers?" He asked it casually, conversationally, but it had far more of an effect on her than it should.

The word *lovers* in his deep, dark voice seemed to travel down her spine, her body trying to remind her of what her brain was desperately trying to forget. Just how good at being lovers they were.

Lorraine Hall is a part-time hermit and full-time writer. She was born with an old soul and her head in the clouds, which, it turns out, is the perfect combination to spend her days creating thunderous alpha heroes and the fierce, determined heroines who win their hearts. She lives in a potentially haunted house with her soulmate and rambunctious band of hermits-in-training. When she's not writing romance, she's reading it.

Books by Lorraine Hall

Harlequin Presents

The Prince's Royal Wedding Demand

Secrets of the Kalyva Crown

Hired for His Royal Revenge
Pregnant at the Palace Altar

Visit the Author Profile page
at Harlequin.com.

Lorraine Hall

A SON HIDDEN FROM THE SICILIAN

(H) HARLEQUIN®
PRESENTS™

Recycling programs
for this product may
not exist in your area.

ISBN-13: 978-1-335-59282-8

A Son Hidden from the Sicilian

Harlequin Enterprises ULC
22 Adelaide St. West, 41st Floor
Toronto, Ontario M5H 4E3, Canada
www.Harlequin.com

Printed in U.S.A.

A SON HIDDEN FROM
THE SICILIAN

CHAPTER ONE

BRIANNA ANDERSEN WATCHED out the window as her airplane touched down in Palermo, Sicily. Her stomach was tied in a million knots while butterflies danced across each and every said knot.

Most of the nerves were excited ones. She was going to show her pieces at an international art show. She would have the opportunity to explore a new place. She was going to attend fancy cocktail parties and hobnob with artists from all over the world. People with too much money were going to bid on her art and this all had the possibility to set her up for life.

All her dreams coming true…in this place she didn't really want them to come true. Because part of her nerves stemmed from worry. Palermo might be a big city, but she knew the chances of seeing *him* were too high. Anything above *no chance at all* was too high, to be honest.

She put him out of her mind as much she could. *If* she had to run into him, she would pretend she barely remembered the summer they'd spent together two years ago in Florence. She, a young artist soaking up all the art and history Italy had to offer. He—well, the version of *him* he'd shown her—a businessman vacationing after a particularly profitable quarter at his company back in his native city of Palermo.

He hadn't mentioned his business was one of the largest and more profitable in Europe. He hadn't mentioned he was its owner and CEO, which made him a *billionaire*. He certainly hadn't told her anything about the hostile takeover his company had accomplished before his little vacation. And most importantly, he'd never told her why he'd abruptly ended things.

He'd simply been there one day, gone the next.

Brianna had been gutted, she could admit that to herself now, though at the time she'd tried to be so sophisticated and strong. But despite the sadness, she had also been philosophical about the whole thing. What artist didn't want some wild, temporary love affair in Florence before returning home to New Jersey? It was very worldly and European after all, and she might have pined a bit while pretending to laugh to her friends back home about her stormy, Italian love affair, but then something…bigger had come along.

In the way of a positive pregnancy test. Suddenly, her feelings about the man mattered less than what she was going to do about the little parting gift he'd left her.

She'd been so determined to tell him. She wanted to laugh at the memory. Bitter though the laugh might have been. There had been a few moments of dreaming up fairy tales, yes. She wasn't immune to wanting a happy-ever-after for a naive little whim she'd indulged herself in.

But then she'd discovered the truth about Lorenzo Parisi. Not just that he was a billionaire. Not just that he'd built an empire from the ground up. But that he was engaged in some sort of feud that had turned violent. On *his* end.

Article after article had painted Lorenzo Parisi as a dangerous, ruthless businessman and billionaire. The accusations had shocked her. At first, she'd refused to believe them. She'd been with him for almost two months and he'd never so much as raised his voice to her or even *near* her.

Could he be intense? Yes. Exacting? Absolutely. Had she ever been *afraid*? Never once.

But how could so many stories be wrong? She'd pored over every story she could find and it was widely accepted he'd been the driving force behind the attack on his rival's *child*. It was that piece of information that had finally gotten through to Brianna.

At the time, her child hadn't felt real to her. Positive test or not, she'd barely had any symptoms. A little exhaustion, a little soreness. She'd only tested because she'd been so late. So, though she understood she was pregnant, it had still been a kind of fanciful knowledge. A dream of what *could* be when she told Lorenzo.

Oddly enough, it was the details of the violent attack on the teenage son of Lorenzo's rival that had made her put her hand on her stomach and finally fully accept that she would grow, and give birth to a *child,* should she so choose and everything went according to plan. The baby wasn't a dream or a fantasy or some possibility. It was a choice to make.

So, in that full realization, she'd come to the conclusion that she could not tell Lorenzo. If this was the truth of him—violence over something as pointless as a few extra dollars when he already had so much—she could not risk herself *and* her child to a ruthless and violent man.

She wouldn't.

So she'd moved in with her parents, kept a low profile, and been blessed with a healthy pregnancy that resulted in a beautiful, wonderful baby boy.

It was only after Gio was born that she'd gotten back into her art again. Something about the sleepless nights and the 24-7 demands of an infant had opened up a *need* for her former creativity, and she'd been fortunate that her involved and helpful parents had never made her or Gio feel like a burden.

Thinking of her parents and Gio, she turned on her phone as the plane finally came to a stop. While everyone bustled around her, Brianna waited for her texts to come through.

When they finally did, she smiled at her phone. All messages from her mother, all photos of Gio. Food-covered face, pulling his grandpa's hair, cheesing for the camera, and in deep, blissful sleep. She felt a pang at each and every one of them.

And still, she couldn't regret coming or leaving

him behind. He was safe and sound under her parents' care and she could focus on why she was here.

Her art. Her career. An opportunity to ensure her parents and Gio never wanted for anything.

And above all else, avoiding Lorenzo Parisi.

Lorenzo Parisi stood in the shadowed corner of the art gallery watching the proceedings with grim amusement. No one approached him. A few looked his way then whispered behind their hands. Most made quite the effort to ignore him.

He let everyone do what they would. He knew there was nothing to be done about public opinion that was already out there. That was why Dante Marino had waged such an impressive media war against him.

Whether Lorenzo denied his involvement in the threats against the Marino family, or got angry about such accusations, or calmly explained how he was not to blame…it did not matter. Dante had bought public opinion. He had centuries of family history and respectability at his fingertips. And he'd used them all to his benefit.

Lorenzo could hardly hold it against the man. If Lorenzo had such things at his disposal, he'd use them, too.

But Lorenzo did not come from a long line of ancestors who'd been paragons of society. He did not have the luxury of generational wealth or connections across decades. He had grown up poor, in charge of far too many mouths to feed, and had scrabbled for every last dime and scrap of power.

Luckily, he was a very good scrabbler, because he had ended up amassing far more than he'd imagined in even his exceptional dreams. Perhaps this was why he could take Dante's lies with a grain of salt. Eventually the man would show a weakness, and Lorenzo would pounce.

He always knew just when to pounce.

Besides, Lorenzo's business continued to succeed. And this was the bottom line. Let Dante wage whatever personality wars he wanted. Lorenzo was interested only in the bottom line.

Of course, tonight his bottom line was a little different than it usually was. He was not here for business. Not here to thumb his nose at all the screaming tabloids or even Dante himself. Though he enjoyed both.

No, his attendance at this art show was about one very specific artist.

And there she was. Not dressed in black like the other artists present. She had never quite fit the stereotype he had in his head of artists as moody, strange, dark and brooding characters.

She was bright. Cheerful. Dreamy. And her art was all of those things, with touches of a kind of whimsical macabre. She painted beautiful landscapes and portraits, then used some kind of embroidery to hint at darker shadows. Bones beneath a dress, blood spilling out of the beautiful earth.

He was not shocked her art had taken off. She

was *unique*, his Brianna, and what did the art world like if not that?

His Brianna. He scowled at that. He had broken things off two years ago when she'd started to get *ideas*, and he had not found those ideas as horrible as he should. He'd been fresh off a business success and it had gone to his head. He could admit that now. He'd gone to Florence for a holiday overly confident, careless enough to make him soft.

But then and now, Lorenzo had a clear plan for his life, and while he had to adapt to certain challenges, detours and surprises, women and relationships would *never* be one of those. Marriage to a struggling American artist did not match his life or business plans, so it had needed to be over.

He'd cut her off and continued to focus on what truly mattered.

Building his empire. Protecting his family.

He had no regrets about that, though the vision of her now threatened that belief. It was as if the entire past two years had evaporated, and he was once again an overly confident fool desperate to have her alone.

Because no one had quite compared to Brianna in the time since he'd left her, and *that* was irritating. That two years later she could appear in the same room as him and he could feel exactly as he had when he'd first laid eyes on her.

Then, she'd been in a museum. Painting. She'd been dressed casually. Jeans and some multicolored sweater with her hair piled up on her head. But unlike the rest of the artists in her group, she'd been focused on her work. The students had been chatting, packing up, and she had been lost in what she'd been creating.

He had been rapt. He'd watched her until she'd finished. Then approached her. Coffee had led to dinner, and then in the blink of an eye two months had gone by and he'd extended his holiday long past when he'd meant to leave.

Sometimes he still wondered if those two months had been a dream. A hallucination. He had certainly not been himself. Maybe she'd cast a spell on him. Sometimes he'd rather believe that than the truth.

Brianna Anderson was remarkable.

She was not dressed so casually tonight—she was wearing a white-and-gold gown that exposed triangles and diamonds of skin at different points. Her eyes were smoky, her hair in long, dark waves around her shoulders. Her cheeks were flushed as she spoke animatedly to a woman dressed from head to toe in black in front of a large piece Lorenzo recognized as Brianna's own artwork at once.

But his gaze kept following the artist herself around the room. She was introduced to different people by the woman in black, and engaged in a variety of conversations over the course of an hour. She carried around a flute of champagne but never took a sip, just worried the stem in her fingers.

Never once did she look his way. Never once did she venture too close to where he still stood in the shadowed corner. He might have thought she simply didn't see him. But it was too convenient—this distance between them at the same party.

So he bided his time. Let some of the people begin to filter out and away. The exhibited pieces were marked as sold—hers more than any other artists. A strange burst of pride settled in his chest that she would be the star tonight.

He supposed it was that pride that had him acting when he'd been determined to just observe this evening. Instead, he approached her. He tried to make some observation about the portrait she was staring so intently at, but he couldn't look away from her. Within reach. He stood there, looking down at her, while she stared resolutely at the painting. As if she didn't sense him here.

He doubted very much that was true.

"Hello, Brianna."

She didn't move. For ticking seconds, she stood perfectly and utterly still. So still it wasn't as if she hadn't heard him. It was as if in fight-or-flight she was stuck at *freeze*.

There should be nothing remarkable about her. She was of average height, size. She had brown hair and blue eyes and a fair complexion. She had the mark of *American* all over her.

And yet...

The fabric of her dress, glittering in gold accents, settled on her curves like poetry. That fair skin seemed imbued with a warmth he'd once felt... and hadn't since, no matter how many women he'd taken to his bed. And the blue of her eyes reminded him of something he could never place but spent far too many hours trying to.

She finally turned her head. She looked up at him, but her expression was politely bland. Her gaze fairly puzzled. "Oh. Hello…" She trailed off purposefully. As if she didn't remember his name.

He laughed. Perhaps it was arrogance. Perhaps it was the fact she was no actress. But he did not for a second believe she'd forgotten him.

"Now, let's not play games, *dusci*. It doesn't suit you."

He'd give her credit. She held his gaze. Didn't cower or even narrow her eyes. She remained looking faintly puzzled. But her cheeks grew darker and darker red. "Lorenzo. It's been a long time," she said after a long, considering moment.

"That it has, Brianna." He smiled at her in the way she had once called *disastrous* to her better judgment.

She did not smile back.

"I… I'm sorry. I have to go." She backed away from him, and he realized she wasn't *really* making eye contact. She was just looking at his forehead as she made a large circle to avoid being with arm's reach. Then she darted for the restrooms.

He watched her go, utterly confused—not a condition he found himself in very often. She looked back at him, once over her shoulder. He did not see any sort of anger in that gaze. This wasn't vitriol in those blue eyes, hatred over the way he'd ended things. It wasn't embarrassment or even some sort of romanticized emotional distress over their long-past breakup.

It was *fear*.

He could understand all the other responses, but even if she'd heard all the rumors about him, fear didn't make sense. All the accusations against him related to the Marino family and business. No woman had ever accused him of violence—though Dante had no doubt tried to pay off a few to. Dante would stop at nothing.

Lorenzo watched the space where Brianna had disappeared. Something was…off. Something was *wrong*.

And he wouldn't rest until he knew what.

CHAPTER TWO

"WELL, THAT WAS very stupid," she muttered to herself as she stared at her reflection in the restroom mirror. Luckily no one else was in here, so she could do things like groan and talk to herself.

Running away was hardly playing it cool. All she'd had to do was stand there and make some small talk, and *then* excuse herself without running.

But coming face-to-face with Lorenzo was like sticking her finger into an electrical socket. No amount of preparation had hardened her against that *zap* of reaction.

She had felt exactly like she had two years ago. Dazzled. Charmed. Tempted. And all he'd done was say hello and accuse her of playing games. What was *wrong* with her?

She sucked in a breath, pulled her phone out of her evening bag and looked at her lock-screen picture. Gio grinning at her from the middle of a clutch of tulips.

She was here for *him*. For everything this show might be able to do for their future. She stared at the picture, usually her guiding star, but in this case all she could see was that he had his father's nose and smile. *Disastrous.*

Yes, Lorenzo was. But she wasn't the same girl she'd been two years ago. She was a mother. She had someone to protect, and she would protect Gio at all costs.

She would *not* feel guilty for keeping Gio from Lorenzo. Not when it could potentially put Gio in danger. Even if it was hard to believe Lorenzo was dangerous, it was clear his business dealings *could* be. And if it could affect his rival's family, why not Lorenzo's own?

She needed to stay away from him. Just by being near him she risked too much, and she was evidently not nearly as clear-sighted as she'd thought she was. So she'd just…go back out and make her excuses to leave. No one needed her here. She'd sold plenty of art so far.

Why was he even here? She didn't allow herself to consider the possibilities because the one she wanted to be true was the one she couldn't want to be true.

He's here to see you.

Well, too bad. She was leaving. She wouldn't give him a chance to… Whatever it was he wanted to do. Even if her heart nearly skipped a beat at the thought of him thinking of her all this time later. Thinking of her and wanting to see her and…

No. There was no *and.* There was only getting out of here so she didn't make any mistakes that might put Gio at risk.

Determined, she slipped her phone back in her purse and marched back out to the gallery. Chin high, shoulders back, *all* determination.

But when she scanned the crowd…she didn't see him. He was gone. She let out a long breath. She felt relief, really.

Really.

It was just it landed strangely like disappointment. And it sat with her. Heavy until she couldn't think past how *exhausted* she was. She found the organizer and said her goodbyes, thanked a few people who complimented her pieces on her way out, and then made her way to the exit, where a car would be waiting to take her back to her hotel.

But before she could get from door to car, there was a slight obstacle.

The man she was trying to avoid.

He stood on the sidewalk, looking up at the beautiful building while Palermo sparkled around them.

She hadn't forgotten the *punch* of him—the figure he cut, all broad-shouldered confidence. Something innate that simply vibrated from him, like a frequency she'd been attuned to since long before she'd met him.

She thought about turning around and running back inside—no matter how stupid that would have been—but his gaze met hers and she found herself frozen—half in the door and half out.

He smiled. *Oh, God.* She was going to end up doing something stupid again. *Think of Gio. Protect your son.*

"Hello again," he offered. "Coming out or scurrying back inside at the sight of me?"

She blinked. She should have a scathing retort. She had known this might happen. She had *prepared* for this. She had even practiced in the mirror all the casual, unbothered, dismissive things she might say to him.

But she had not prepared for everything she'd felt back then to come rushing back. Slithering through all the cracks in her armor so she felt like an exposed wire—sensitive and dangerous. On the verge of something terribly *explosive*.

"Are you afraid of me, *dusci*?" he all but purred. "I must admit, I cannot imagine why," he said with a silky arrogance that helped break through the haze affecting her.

"You can't?" she returned, finally finding her voice in her irritation with him. She forced herself to step outside, though she kept by the door. She would have an escape if she needed one. "When rumors swirl about you the way they do? None of them good?"

There was the *tiniest* flicker of something in his expression. Not aggression, but that intensity she'd once been enthralled by. *You still are.*

"Tell me, Brianna. Do you believe every rumor you hear, or only ones about former lovers?" He asked it casually, *conversationally*, but it had far more of an effect on her than it should.

The word *lovers* in his deep, dark voice seemed to travel down her spine, her body trying to remind her of what her brain was desperately trying to forget. Just how good at *lovers* they were.

Gio. Think of Gio. But that wasn't exactly helpful, because as much as she wanted to protect her son—more than *anything*—she couldn't fully absolve herself enough to not feel guilt over the situation.

This man did not know he had a son at all. He'd never been on the receiving end of Gio's smiles or held the boy as he'd grown.

Because he's a violent criminal, Brianna. Because he deals in dangerous things that could hurt your son. This is not your fault.

"I haven't seen one article or media story to refute any of these claims against you," Brianna replied, determined to keep her position even as he stepped closer. She would not let him physically intimidate her. "Never saw *you* attempt to refute it, in fact."

He cocked his head, reached out and touched a finger to her cheek. His gaze was focused on that finger, and he slid it down the length of her jaw. The touch arced through her like electricity. She shuddered and knew she shouldn't. She *yearned* and knew she couldn't.

This was no intimidation. It was seduction. She'd been down this road once before. She had to be smarter than she'd been two years ago. Stronger.

"My original statement refuted it," he said, his voice low, serious. His dark gaze matched it.

And it was basically a lie. "That was your publicist." She should move. Step away from his wandering finger. Not let him block out the light. Block out her sanity.

"You are *very* abreast of this. I didn't realize the dealings of a Sicilian businessman would make news in America."

"You're hardly *just* a Sicilian businessman. Which I did not find out until I got home."

Home. Gio. Get out of here, Brianna.

She finally got her mind to get through to her body enough to move—sidestep away from his shadow, his finger, his orbit. She began to stride toward the car that would take her to safety.

She had to be safe. For Gio. Safe and smart and… protect Gio at all costs. Which meant protecting herself.

"I thought we could have coffee. Catch up."

She stopped midstride because was he *insane?* But she didn't look back at him, just forced herself to continue walking. "It was never just coffee with us, Lorenzo."

He chuckled as he matched her stride easily, the sound deep and warm as it settled inside of her like a drug. Only a drug could make her want something she knew was far too dangerous. "That would be enjoyable as well."

Those words hit a little hard. Not just because they were tempting, and she hated herself that they were, but because she'd been busy preparing for motherhood and then being a single mother for the past two years. She had not *enjoyed* anything remotely sexual in so long she had begun to wonder if she even had those kinds of desires anymore.

Leave it to Sicily and Lorenzo to remind her that she did.

But it was *infuriating*, really, to be tempted by so little. He hadn't apologized for breaking things off with her abruptly. He hadn't even acknowledged that two years had passed. He was just…propositioning her, like that was all he *had* to do.

"I won't be having coffee with you. Or anything else, Lorenzo."

"Why not?"

Why not. *Why not?* She whirled on him, a surprising anger spurting up inside her. Surprising because she'd convinced herself she was over this. That by keeping Gio a secret she had somehow gotten even with him. But the emotion stirred, even years later, from him flirting with her like he'd done nothing wrong, like nothing had changed…

"You lied to me. You deserted me. Abruptly and without explanation. We can chalk that all up to a naive art student on her first international trip being easily charmed by a suave businessman who knows the games people play and plays them oh so well. Fine enough. But I'm not that woman anymore. And I'm not in any position to have random flings with men who have so little depth or human decency."

Lorenzo did not allow his temper to flare, though the shot about his *decency* landed sharp enough to make his control a hard-won thing. But he held on to the shield. He carefully iced the anger and offense away. He even smiled. Because there was something underneath her words he couldn't quite understand or guess at.

She was behaving…strangely. Like she had something to hide. Like he was someone to fear. None of that added up, even if she was angry with him, still, for his…abrupt breakup two years ago. "Why not?"

She blinked, clearly caught off guard. "Why not what?"

"Why are you not in a position to engage in 'random flings' with men you once enjoyed?" *Enjoyed* seemed a dim word for what sparked between them—then, now—but he didn't wish to overplay his hand.

Her mouth opened, but no sound came out. He saw her struggle to come up with an answer.

"Married?"

He watched her carefully. Once again she didn't speak right away. Was she considering lying? And what would be the lie?

More important, what was the truth? Why did it *need* a lie?

Well, he'd find out soon enough. He'd know everything there was to know about Brianna Andersen over the past two years and her strange behavior in the here and now.

She straightened her shoulders, lifted her chin, and met his gaze with direct blue eyes. Not like the sky or the ocean or even a flower. Just a shade that haunted him still.

"Lorenzo, we had a brief affair years ago," she said, and she sounded tired though she didn't look it. "I'm sure you've enjoyed many a model, actress, and who knows what all since then."

"You really *have* been paying attention, Brianna."

Her mouth firmed. "Some drugs are hard to kick, Lorenzo. But I won't be returning to this one. So I'd appreciate it if you leave me alone."

He couldn't quite keep his smile in place at her treating him like he was some kind of drooling stalker. A *drug*, when he knew the utter destruction those could do. "I do not stick around where I'm not wanted."

"You don't even stick around where you *are* wanted," she shot back.

And here was the anger he'd maybe expected. Or thought he deserved for his abrupt goodbye. The scorned woman. Still, no matter if it was deserved or not, he didn't *appreciate* her little barbs. "What is it you want from me, Brianna?"

"An apology would prove to me that you're a better man than I think you are, but the fact of the matter is, it'd have to be genuine. And begged-for apologies don't tend to be genuine. So I don't want anything from you, Lorenzo. Except to be left alone."

"I am not sorry for what I did." It had been necessary. He didn't do things that weren't *essential*.

Except you're standing here right now having this ridiculous conversation.

"Fantastic. Regardless, I'm not here for an apology. I'm here to sell my art. In a few days, I'll go home. I had no intention of running into you, asking for apologies, or dealing with you at all. You're a piece of ancient history and I'd like to leave it that way."

She stood there, delivering these statements with an anger and bitterness he never would have guessed existed inside of someone so…warm. But she had not only been warmth and sweetness. Even then. That was the problem with Brianna.

There were so many facets to her. She was an easy woman to read, and yet not an easy woman to get to know. Because she could be strong and she could be vulnerable. Naive and innocent. Cynical and passionate. He could see all these things on her face as easily as the makeup she wore—and yet it did not mean he understood the *whys* behind all her feelings, or that he could predict them. She'd gone from ignoring him, to being skittish, to an exhausted kind of rejection of him in a handful of minutes, and he understood very few of these abrupt changes.

But they were all her. Not acts. Not games. Just… her.

Perhaps that was the secret of why she'd lingered in his mind even after he'd left her. Even after he'd spent considerable time trying to cut her out of his memory.

She was an unfixable problem. A jumbled puzzle that would never have all the pieces. He couldn't herd her into one of his boxes, even though he desperately wanted to.

Needed to.

Otherwise she existed in his brain like some sort of evil spell. Constantly hovering and poking at him. Two years. No one haunted Lorenzo Parisi for *two years* and simply dismissed him with a few harsh words.

No more than he would continue to chase someone who had made it quite clear she wished him to remain history. *He* was in control of himself. In control of everything.

So he didn't follow her as she walked to the car. He didn't demand to know where she was staying. He didn't press his advantage—which he knew he still held, from the way she reacted to him when he'd done little more than touch her with the tip of his finger.

He let her go.

But that didn't mean he was done with Brianna Andersen.

Or she him.

CHAPTER THREE

BRIANNA HAD BEEN dead set on leaving early. Going home to safety, half a world away from Lorenzo Parisi.

Then she had gotten back to her hotel room and spoken with her parents. The video call with them and Gio calmed her. It eased those jagged edges inside of her. She had all this to go home to. And all this to succeed for.

So she'd gone to bed knowing that going home now would be a failure. There was still one more art showing and a cocktail party that her manager had insisted could be a place to make lasting partnerships. It was a few more days and surely she wasn't so cowardly as to run home after one uncomfortable encounter.

She had woken up the next morning determined she would attend all these events as promised. She'd gone about her day certain she could handle it. If Lorenzo continued to appear…

She closed her eyes now as she sat on her hotel bed, procrastinating getting ready for this evening's party. She needed more time to herself for the memory of her encounter with Lorenzo to fade, but she didn't have that.

She would have to find a way to be stronger in the face of him. It was will power. It was strength. He wasn't threatening her. He didn't pose a *threat* to anything other than her peace of mind and that was *her* problem. Certainly not his.

Besides, if he continued to harass her, she could always call the police. If he was capable of violence against his rival's *child*, then surely the police would listen to her and do…something.

Surely.

She shook her head. This was catastrophic thinking. It wouldn't come to that. Maybe Lorenzo had attended last night's art show because she would be there, but he lived in Palermo. It was likely a lark. To see if she was still so easily beddable.

And she *wasn't*. Maybe she'd *felt* temptation, but she had not given in to it. Gold star for her.

If only she could trust herself to *maintain* such a stance. She closed her eyes, rubbed her temples. She really needed to get ready. She needed to trust herself. She needed to find all that strength she'd honed since Gio had come into her world.

Or perhaps feign illness and make arrangements to go home. Was the potential for a big payout more important than her sanity? She could be back in New Jersey with her son by tomorrow. She'd get a job at the grocery store. At the local school district. She could drive a bus. Or serve sloppy joes to high school kids. She could do *anything* other than…

Follow your dreams? Give up everything you've worked for because of some man?

"Ugh," she said. Out loud. Letting the sound echo off the walls. Here she was in Sicily, selling her art, and she couldn't even enjoy herself because she'd had one short-sighted affair two years ago. That was hardly the kind of woman she wanted to be.

But before she could determine exactly *what* kind of woman she wanted to be in this situation, she heard the telltale noise of a door being opened.

Her door.

She got up off the bed, more puzzled than leery at first. Until she saw the man enter her room. As though he could. As though he *should*.

For a moment, she only gaped. But that didn't stop his forward movement, even as he closed the door behind him. He came right into the main area of her hotel room, glaring at her the whole way.

"What are you doing here? How did you get in? I…" She backed away as he got closer. Put the expansive bed between them as if that would somehow save her. "I'll…call security," she said, her voice a panicked whisper more than a decisive or threatening shout.

He did not change course. Did not look the least bit concerned. Simply gestured for the phone she now stood close to. "Be my guest."

She stared at him, mouth open, heart pounding. This was threatening behavior, after all, but he didn't *act* like he was threatening her. He took a seat on the armchair in the corner like he was just going to… wait for her to make the call.

She grabbed the phone and punched the number for the front desk. When the cheerful woman answered, Brianna stumbled over her words, but she got them out. "A…a man has barged into my room. I need the police. I need…"

"No worries, Ms. Andersen," the attendant said, none of her cheerful customer service voice changing in concern. "Mr. Parisi has assured me his team can handle any disruption. You're in very good hands."

She looked at the man in question. Who lounged in her hotel room chair like he had every right. But he was a *billionaire*. He'd clearly told the hotel staff some…story. And now what? Who did she call? What did she do?

Well, she wasn't just going to *take* it. Carefully, she replaced the phone in its receiver. "What are you doing?" Brianna demanded, clutching the ends of the robe together as her mind whirled. Was there anything in this room she could use as a weapon? Was she justified in using a weapon when all he'd done so far was sit there?

Well, he *had* broken into her room. That was against the law.

Right?

"We need to have a discussion, Brianna," he said. Like they were sitting in a meeting room talking about a contract or business merger.

But they were in her hotel room. She was barefoot

in a robe, with her damp hair piled on the top of her head. Which struck her as an unfair disadvantage when he sat there in a suit looking like he owned the whole world. "Yes, normal discussions happen when people break into other people's hotel rooms." She considered the lamp, but it was still plugged into the wall. There was no way she could unplug it and throw it at him before he did something. Except...he *wasn't* doing anything except sitting there.

There were no smiles like last night, she noted. Everything about him was serious. Businesslike.

"You have a child," he said. Flatly. Without emotion.

But she saw the fury in his gaze. He did not make a move. He sat there as calmly and leisurely as if they were sitting down to tea. But the temper was all there in his dark eyes.

She swallowed. Her gaze darted toward the door. She could crawl over the bed and run for the door, but would she be fast enough?

"You can run, Brianna. I will not hurt you, but I will follow." He stood, slowly and menacingly even though he'd just said he wouldn't hurt her. "You have a child, Brianna."

"So you keep saying." He didn't make a move for her, and something about that very fact kept her from lunging over the bed. No matter how angry he was, he wasn't trying to hurt her.

That doesn't mean he won't. Don't be an idiot.

"A son," he continued in that calm, even voice she

assumed worked *very* well in whatever fancy board-rooms he frequented. "Born in July of last year."

"I don't know—"

"Think very carefully, *dusci*, before you lie to me." *This* was laced with anger. With a sharp-edged viciousness that had her swallowing and fighting the desire to cower.

And still, he kept his distance. Just stood by the chair, looking at her like she was a trail of slime. Too low to even bother to hurt.

"I haven't lied to you, Lorenzo." She tried to fall back on her own outrage. Her own sense of betrayal, hollow though it was in the moment. "I know the same cannot be said of *you*, but that does not make *me* a liar."

"You have kept something from me, then. You prefer secrets to lies. I prefer the truth. Did you give birth to *my* son on your return to America?"

"I don't know what concern it is of yours."

He was very quiet. The kind of silence that grew heavy as it stretched out. She felt no need to break it. There was nothing to say. *Somehow* he'd found her secret. And she did not know how to change the course of that except curse herself for ever coming here. For thinking she could have success and creative fulfillment *and* be safe from her secret getting out.

This was Lorenzo's fault—for leaving her, for ordering violent attacks, for being here—but it was also her own for putting herself in this foolish situation all for the sense of freedom selling her art had provided her.

She should have known one person didn't get too much of a good thing. She had wonderful parents, a beautiful son. It should have been enough. Shame on her for wanting more.

"Here is how the rest of your time in Palermo will go," Lorenzo said matter-of-factly. Whatever anger had slipped into his voice earlier had now chilled. "You will attend tonight's party, as I am told it is very important for your career. You will attend your final showing in a few days. Then we will fly to New Jersey, together, and you will take me to *my* son, Brianna. As you should have done long before now."

She did not care for his bossy tone. For the formality of it. Like she was an employee or a subordinate. He had never spoken to her like this before, and it was enough to put her back up. No matter how ill-advisedly.

"I have done *everything* to protect my son and I will never, *ever* stop. You are a violent criminal. No doubt if you weren't a billionaire, you'd be in jail."

He laughed then, but not the same chuckle from last night. Nothing that spoke of levity. It was dark and it was bitter.

"I would think this would go without saying, but if it needs to be said, so be it. I have *never* ordered anyone be hurt in my name, Brianna. I am not a coward. If I wished to attack my rival, I would attack him—not a *child*—with my own two bare hands."

She could picture it. Which did not send the sharp

bolt of fear through her as it should. "Is that supposed to make me feel better?" she asked instead.

"I do not care how *you* feel. I care that my son breathes, even as we speak, and I have never once laid eyes on him or held him. That every choice about his life has been kept from me. My own flesh and blood. I care that you are the architect of this betrayal."

"Betrayal? Betrayal is being left without a word. Without a second glance. Betrayal is being *abandoned*. You lied to me, time and time again."

"You knew who I was."

"No, I did not, Lorenzo. Not how you mean. Your name, your body, the man you wanted me to think you were, yes, but not the business, the billionaire status, the cruelty in the name of it. I was going to tell you about the pregnancy, but first I had to find out how to reach you—because you'd certainly left me no ability to do so. And all I found was story after story about how the father of my child was a cruel, dangerous man."

"Do you think I would hurt my own flesh and blood? Is this how little you think of the men you invite into your bed?"

"Who was I supposed to believe, Lorenzo? The man who'd left me high and dry after two months of lies, or a series of stories that no one refuted except your publicist, with a tepid statement I knew you had nothing to do with."

"You were supposed to inform me I had a son."

"No. A mother's job is to protect her son. No

matter what. *That* is what I did." Even now, hearing him deny the accusations against him and believing him—whether she should or not—she knew she'd done the right thing. Protecting Gio was all that could ever matter.

But guilt settled in her gut like acid at the way he'd said, "*I care that my son breathes, even as we speak, and I have never once laid eyes on him or held him.*"

With such barely contained emotion she could only think how *horrible* it would have been to have missed all Gio's firsts. Those sleepless nights, the gurgling smiles, the warmth of a baby's cuddle.

It made her want to soften, apologize, insist they fly home right now so he could meet his son.

But this couldn't happen. She had to protect Gio. And until she knew for certain her child would be safe from the violence surrounding this man, she had to do whatever she could to keep them apart.

Lorenzo did not have a temper. Anger and impetuousness had never served him well, so he'd never allowed himself outbursts. The oldest of ten, he'd had to learn at a very young age—so young he barely remembered—how to be responsible, how to control what he felt, how to put others first when they needed it.

In a house full of hungry mouths, many had needed it.

But his family was no longer destitute. He had more money than a god. He enjoyed his work, his life, and didn't allow himself very often to consider the fear and pain of growing up the way he had.

But ever since his investigator had brought him news of this child this afternoon, he'd been reminded of the darkest times in his life. The anger that threatened to take hold and destroy everything he held dear.

He had a son. The child was over a year old. Walking and no doubt doing some talking—Lorenzo was well versed in child development. He'd helped raise most of his youngest siblings from diapers to adulthood—and he had not known his own son existed.

Anger, sharp and dark and dangerous, swirled inside of him like its own entity. The only time he could remember feeling this furious before was a time he never let himself consider. Memories too painful to ever address.

How dare this woman bring them up in him.

"You should get dressed or we will be late," he said to her. In cool, calm tones because he was in control. He was in charge of *everything*.

Except the boy she's kept from you.

She stared at him, still clutching the edges of her fluffy hotel robe together. As if it were armor that would save her. He could force her to miss the party, the art show in a few days. It would be her just due to miss these opportunities for her career.

But that would be needlessly cruel, and while he might be all for that on a personal level, he also knew what it was to be the child of a parent who grew more and more bitter with the other. Who blamed and manipulated and used and hurt.

He would not give that to his child.

On the other hand, he could leave Brianna here and fly to New Jersey himself and lay claim to the boy.

But he would not put his son through anything that might scar him. Arriving a stranger without the boy's mother would not be what was best for the child. Even if Brianna deserved to miss two years of their son's life in retribution.

Someday, he would find a way to punish her. But it would not be at his child's expense. Never.

He would give Brianna one thing. The vehement way she spoke of protecting her child at any cost was good. He could even admit—at least in the privacy of his thoughts—he imagined she was a good mother. It was that warmth, that nurturing she'd shown him two years ago she no doubt showered on her own child.

But that did not excuse her actions. Protection did not excuse them either. Believing paparazzi fodder and unfounded accusations was…

Betrayal.

She stood there, daring to look like *she* had been the one betrayed. Still not making a move to get dressed. Still not offering any groveling apologies. Just standing there, far too tempting with her bare legs and feet and big blue eyes full of conflicting emotions—none of them sharp enough.

Brianna had never been much of a sharp edge. It

was one of the things that had drawn him to her. That infinite softness. *A good thing for a mother to have.*

Mother. The mother of his child. A child he did not know. He had his reasons for not rushing off to meet this boy. The one he liked least was the conflicting emotions that threatened to rule him.

He would not meet his son in such a state—no matter how he ached to hold his flesh and blood.

No, he would be in complete control. He would map out every move. By the end of Brianna's time in Palermo, he would be ready. He would have everything under control.

Including Brianna.

Who still had not moved.

"I don't understand what you're doing," she said at last. "Why... Why aren't we going to New Jersey right now?"

He looked down at her, shoving the anger down underneath all the ways he'd learned to control it. "You should understand, recognize it, if you are a good enough mother. That now that I know his existence, every step I take will be in making certain my son has the life he deserves. Which, much as I may despise it, involves a mother who is not miserable. You will have your career highlight, Brianna. *I* certainly won't be the one to stop it." He made a big show of looking at his watch. "Now. Let's not waste any more time. I believe you have patrons to woo."

CHAPTER FOUR

BRIANNA WAS HARDLY cognizant of getting ready, though that was just what she did. Dressed. Put on makeup and did her hair. On the surface, she looked exactly as she was meant to—the American artist eager to make connections.

But surface hid so much.

She sucked in a slow, long breath, then let it out twice as slowly. Lorenzo sat next to her in the car, a living, breathing rock of absolutely no reaction whatsoever. In the dark of the car, she couldn't see his eyes, but she imagined the anger still lurked there.

He hadn't lost his temper. There'd been no threats, not really. He'd laid down the law—his law—sure, but it wasn't… Maybe he would have become violent if she'd argued, if she'd refused. Maybe he had that in him…

But she was having a harder and harder time believing it. He was a proud man. Sending someone to do his dirty work…it did not fit what she knew of him at all. And even if he was ruthless enough to harm someone else in his business affairs, he would never harm a child.

That much she'd gathered from his choices tonight.

Had she made a mistake two years ago? She closed her eyes. It didn't matter. She'd acted in her son's best interest. If that had been a mistake, so be it. Better safe than sorry and Gio's safety would always trump everything.

She had only a few days to decide what that looked like.

The car rolled up to the beautiful old building the cocktail party would take place in. Beyond it, the sun was setting, lighting up Mount Pellegrino. The city itself beginning to sparkle to life as night began to fall.

Brianna took another deep breath and tried to remind herself that even with this unfortunate turn of events, she should enjoy her time here. Somehow.

She did not look at Lorenzo, knew she would not be able to keep her facade if she did. "I do not think we should enter together," she said as regally and coolly as she could manage.

He said nothing for a long, stretched-out minute. Then he sighed. As if she was very, very dim. "If you think you are leaving my sight before we leave for America, you are sorely mistaken. I will be by your side through every moment of this party. I have a staff member packing your hotel room for you as we speak. You will be staying at my residence until we leave."

She whipped her head to face him now, anger overtaking worry. He'd sent staff to pack *her* things? "It did not occur to you to *ask*?"

"No, it did not. Because there is nothing to *ask* of you, Brianna. You have done everything the way *you* wanted since you learned of *our* son. Now it is my turn to approach things as I want. Luckily, we can both agree to put the child first."

It was a slapdown that landed because it was true. She had, in fact, chosen everything. She would put Gio first, always. But she didn't think he got to claim he would too at this point. "You haven't even asked his name."

Lorenzo's expression was hard as granite and betrayed nothing. "I know his name. Where he was born. His height, his weight. I know everything now."

She swallowed as a strange kind of shame washed over her—when she should be *afraid* he could get all that information without her permission. She had nothing to be ashamed of. But knowing this didn't seem to change the course of her emotions.

"You could have asked," she pointed out. She might have kept Gio's existence a secret, but he could have had *some* understanding. He could have come to her with something other than all this controlled anger and self-important orders.

Or so she told herself to keep from crying. Or, worse, begging his forgiveness. When she refused to apologize for what she'd done, because it had been the *right* thing, even if the stories were wrong.

"You could have told me of his existence," Lorenzo replied evenly. "Even last night. You had ample opportunity. Yet you chose to keep him from me."

"Imagine that. That when I learned I was pregnant after being so coldly discarded, and decided I wanted to have this child, that discovering the man I'd shared my body and heart with had lied to me. Had hidden his true identity." But that wasn't why she'd kept Gio a secret, was it? Because she'd still been ready to tell Lorenzo, to hope for some kind of reconciliation no matter how hurt she was. Because love made a woman stupid.

But a child did not. "And still I would have told you," she said, though it was embarrassing to share the truth. But it was necessary he understand this wasn't about her. It was never about *her*. "Until I learned you were engaged in some kind of business battle that would leave a child harmed. Now, whether this is true or not, does it matter? What I read was that a child was hurt. And I would not allow the same to happen to my child."

"You can be angry at the way things ended for us, Brianna, but you know I am not the sort of man to hurt my own."

"No. I *thought* I knew that. Then I learned everything I thought I knew about you was a lie. Why shouldn't your lack of violence be a lie too?"

His jaw was tight, and frustration flashed in those dark eyes. "Not a lie," he gritted out.

"What is it you said last night? Not a lie, but you kept something from me. Lots of somethings. You claim to prefer the truth, but you hid everything you were. So I couldn't trust anything I might have felt."

"A simple internet search when we were together would have told you everything. I was hardly engaging in back-alley machinations to keep you from discovering more about me."

"But I didn't search, Lorenzo. Because I trusted you." She looked away from him then because she hated reliving this pain in front of him. And it had been painful. More painful than she cared to admit to herself. Because she had loved him. Deeply. Immovably.

And he'd deserted her without a second glance. She had been that unimportant to him. "More the fool me, I know," she murmured, staring at the glittering building people were pouring into, glittering themselves like so many jewels.

She didn't belong here.

But she *was* here, and here was an opportunity. "I did what I thought was best. I always will when it comes to Gio," she said, calm and detached, she liked to think. "You can be angry about it. You have every right to be. But it changes nothing. Not what happened, not how I feel."

Lorenzo's door opened. He didn't move right away. His gaze was on her, opaque and unreadable, for what felt like forever. Then he moved, sliding out of the car.

Brianna let out a long breath she had not been fully aware of holding. Holding her breath. Holding her own. She was managing and she had to keep managing, but it was a hard-won thing.

Her door opened, and Lorenzo stood there, still a figure that took her breath away. She knew what he would look like without the jacket, the tie. With the buttons unbuttoned, with his hands in her hair and his mouth hard and demanding. Or soft and exploratory. She knew what it would feel like to slide her hand into his as she now had to do.

With all that had happened in two years between them shooting barbs and reigniting old hurts. And still she knew the contact would spread through her like warmth and want.

She steeled herself and then took the hand he offered to help her out of the car. She looked up at Lorenzo and held that dark gaze, determined to be as strong and angry as he was. "I will do everything to protect my son. Right now, I'm trying to believe that you would too. The minute I don't—I don't care what billions you have, what power—I will do *everything and anything* to protect him from you if you or your business poses a threat. And I mean *anything*. So perhaps you should take a pause in hating me and blaming me and look inward and make sure nothing you've done will follow you and land on Gio's doorstep."

Lorenzo stood there, Brianna's hand in his, her blazing anger focused solely on him. She clearly had no idea how easily he could crush her. With his money. With his power. *He* had all the control.

And yet she stood up to him, all naive confidence that she could best him simply because she wanted to.

This was not the woman he remembered. How soft she'd been back then. Eager. There'd been passion in her, but it had been open. Enthusiastic. Not this sharp-edged force of nature determined to protect something at all costs.

Worse than this surprising new side to her, which did *nothing* to ease the lustful turn of thoughts that even now he was fighting off, was the fact that she was right. Regardless of his power or his money, there *was* the chance he was a threat to his own son.

There was a tiny, minuscule sense of rightness to her keeping his son from him. Protecting this boy he'd never met nor laid eyes on. Because even though he had not ordered the attack on Dante's son, Dante clearly thought he had.

And that made Dante dangerous. Just because he hadn't retaliated yet did not mean he wouldn't. Particularly if he found out that Lorenzo had a son of his own.

Brianna raised an eyebrow at him now. A silent look that said, *Are we going to go in or stand here and stare at each other all night?*

She'd rattled him with this idea that *he* was an inadvertent threat. When nothing in his adult life had been inadvertent.

Except everything to do with her.

He pushed all these whirling thoughts aside, tucked her soft arm into his and moved them toward the building. A cocktail party was the last thing he wanted to deal with right now, but he knew how to compartmentalize. How to do that which he wanted for the greater good.

While *he* did not care about Brianna's dream or talent, their son no doubt would, as he grew. Lorenzo would never be the tool Brianna used to turn their son against him. He would ensure Brianna had *every* opportunity she desired. If he had to charm everyone at this party himself.

They entered, were greeted by the organizers, and Lorenzo didn't miss the speculative glances. The whispers in their wake. Perhaps he should not have had them arrive together, but he didn't trust her not to bolt.

He'd find her. No matter what. But this all worked better, would go smoother, if they did things his exact way.

His exact way was always best.

Or so he'd always thought. Until they moved into the buzzing room full of people and drinks and art and Lorenzo caught a glimpse of the last man he wanted to see here.

Dante. Over in a corner, laughing with a few other businessmen Lorenzo recognized as clients of Marino & Family Industries.

A dangerous temper swept through him. All those swirling feelings of anger, of indignation, of hate. This man was trying to ruin everything the Parisi name stood for, and it was worse now. Before it had just been him.

Now it was his son.

There was no reason Dante should be here. No reason at all. Except to bother Lorenzo in some way, and Lorenzo had a terrible feeling *this* was what his publicist had been chattering at him about that he'd been ignoring. Something about pictures in the paper. He'd been so focused on discovering he'd had a son that he hadn't paid any mind. There were *always* pictures of him splashed about after he attended an event.

Now he wondered if those pictures had included Brianna.

Brianna. Here and on his arm, while that pit viper turned his attention from his cronies to Lorenzo across the room.

No.

Lorenzo maneuvered Brianna into a corner. "You'll have to excuse me, *dusci*. I must talk to this odious businessman. Why don't you go make your necessary artist rounds?"

"I thought I wasn't to leave your side." She didn't say this in disappointment, but in suspicion. Her eyes narrowed as she studied his face.

He could not let her in on the danger Dante posed. It would complicate things. So he lifted her hand, brushed his mouth over the knuckles, making sure to keep eye contact. Holding her hand gently until a faint blush crept into her cheeks.

"Ah, but I trust you, my sweet Brianna."

The flush on her cheeks deepened so much that

desire twined with satisfaction for having put her off guard.

He turned away from her, to head Dante off at the pass. He didn't look back at Brianna. It would give away too much to both his rival and the woman in question.

He met Dante halfway between the man's initial starting point and Brianna. "Hello, Dante," he greeted jovially, as it always set the man on edge when Lorenzo refused to deal in anger or veiled threats.

But tonight Dante only smiled. "Why have you sent off your companion? I wished to compliment the artist on her…alluring work."

Lorenzo did not outwardly react. Such sad little provocations didn't tend to work on him quite so effectively, but he would blame the roiling anger inside of him on the fact everything had changed this morning when his investigator had delivered the news.

"I did not know you were such a fan of the arts, Dante," Lorenzo offered with a smile that was likely sharper than it should be. "But I'm sure your compliments can be given by way of buying a piece."

"I was thinking more of funding the artist herself." Dante sipped his drink. "She's beautiful. American, a pity, but beautiful."

Lorenzo knew the emotions vying for purchase were more complicated than just hating this man. Something darker, with claws. Something far too close to *jealousy*. And a wave of old concerns that he would never, *ever* have again. Because no matter what he'd done or not done in his life, he would never allow himself to sink into the pain and suffering of his parents.

He was connected to Brianna now. He had a son. It left him too close to all the mistakes they'd made. But he was stronger.

Better.

"Perhaps you should better fund your staff, Dante. Last I heard there was quite the labor squabble in your offices in Rome. Best to focus your funding there, I should say."

Dante's self-satisfied expression flickered, but only for a moment. Which had Lorenzo bracing himself.

"There's quite a hubbub around you today," Dante continued, his eyes lingering on Brianna as she toured the room, led by her manager.

"Is there?" Lorenzo returned, thankful his voice could sound bored when his blood boiled and every effort right now was going to repressing old memories of his mother. What she had done. What she had lost. To men like Dante. All because his father had not been man enough to put his family first.

All because of *love*.

Lorenzo would correct these mistakes. Always.

"Last night you made quite the splash slobbering all over the American artist," Dante continued.

Lorenzo laughed, though he felt no mirth. Still, the little accusation made it easier to focus on the present. "Ah, Dante, your talent for exaggeration knows no bounds. Slobbering? Honestly. Even the paparazzi couldn't come up with such a story."

Dante shrugged philosophically. "I was certainly interested. Interested to go digging. You've met the artist before, have you? In Florence."

Lorenzo could not keep *all* emotion off his face. That shouldn't be easy-to-find knowledge, and who could confirm it? At Dante's grin of satisfaction Lorenzo knew his cold fury was echoing off him. A point for Dante, indeed, but a man could lose the battle and win the war.

Lorenzo would win this war.

"I'm deeply touched you would go through all the trouble to look into this for me, Dante. With so many labor disputes going on at Marino, you would think *that* would take up all your time and concern. How kind you would spare some for me."

Dante's expression didn't even flicker this time. He only smiled wider. "Gio is a nice name. Isn't it?"

For a moment, all Lorenzo heard was a faint buzzing in his ears. He could picture moving forward. Putting his hands on Dante's throat and squeezing.

But he did not do this. For two reasons. One, he had the sinking suspicion Dante wanted him to. No doubt to aid in the rumors Lorenzo was a vicious monster.

Second, he saw Brianna. Watching him with a frown of faint puzzlement on her face. Her opinion of him didn't matter at all, but he had plans. A vision for the future.

Maybe she'd thrown him a curveball, but he'd

already recalibrated. He knew what his life with a son looked like.

Now he just had to recalibrate again. Because Dante's curveball was nothing short of a threat.

"It seems congratulations are in order, Lorenzo. Though a confirming birth certificate seems to be missing. But that would suit you, wouldn't it?" Dante clapped him on the back and smiled. "Hurt my child. Ignore your own. The press will love it. They're probably halfway to New Jersey as we speak."

And then he walked away.

CHAPTER FIVE

BRIANNA WATCHED AS Lorenzo spoke to a man. Older, shorter, his dark hair sprinkled with gray and his smile not warm or kind at all, but the fact he was smiling at all made the whole thing seem...worse.

The look of pure fury on Lorenzo's face was what held her attention though. She watched as Lorenzo's hand curled into a tight fist in reaction to whatever the man said.

Brianna was frozen in space, hearing none of the conversation going on around her. She was sure she was about to see all that violence Lorenzo had been accused of on public display, and then she'd have to escape somehow. Get back to New Jersey, get Gio, then erase her entire identity...somehow, and then what?

But Lorenzo never moved. Just stood very still as the man spoke once more, clapped him on the back and then strode away. Lorenzo did not watch him leave. He did nothing for a few ticking seconds. Then his gaze moved.

And found her.

He did not immediately cross the room, as she'd thought he might, based on the sheer force of his gaze. Instead, he moved in a circular kind of path. Talking to this person, taking a canapé from that tray, taking his time.

Always coming for her. No matter whom she talked to, no matter how many sips of wine she took, she was far too aware he was headed for her.

Once he finally arrived, he slid his arm through hers as if they were still lovers instead of veritable strangers who basically hated one another.

She hated that she wished for the first.

He leaned close, his mouth at her ear. She would *not* shudder. She would *not* react. "We must leave at once."

Brianna might have argued, but she didn't particularly want to be here. She couldn't concentrate on any conversation with Lorenzo circling like a shark, and she liked even less the man he'd been talking to, whose eyes were on her everywhere she went.

She'd spoken to some people, made her rounds. Her manager wouldn't be too happy with an early exit, but a migraine was beginning to pound behind her eyes and she needed space. Time. To think.

"All right."

If he was surprised at her easy agreement, he didn't act it. He kept that pleasant fake smile on his face and maneuvered them toward the exit. When they reached her manager, Brianna didn't lie exactly. She explained she had a migraine and she needed some dark and some quiet to recover.

Once they were outside, everything about Lorenzo changed. His scowl was hard, his eyes harder. There was no mask, only fury.

His car and driver were already waiting for them right at the entrance. Worry began to displace her own discomfort.

"Lorenzo, what's going on?"

He didn't so much as look at her. Simply opened the car door and gestured her inside. When she did not get in, he turned that ferocious scowl on her and leaned close.

"We must retrieve Gio at once."

Terror pierced her soul. "What's happened?"

He nudged her into the car and in her shocked state she had no fight in her. Gio. She had to get to Gio. That was all that mattered.

"The press knows," Lorenzo said quickly as he pulled the door closed behind him. The driver immediately pulled away from the curb.

"Knows what?"

He spared her a look, again like she was dim. "That I have a son. In New Jersey."

Brianna blinked, trying to find the terrible threat in those words. But they were only the truth. She frowned as she tried to calm her racing heart.

"We will collect him," Lorenzo was staying. "We will take him to my estate."

"Your *estate*? Here?"

"Outside Palermo, but yes, in Sicily. It is protected. No one will have access to him. I assume the same cannot be said of your home in America."

Brianna shook her head as if this would make the jumble of thoughts going on inside her coalesce into something rational. Something that made sense.

But the only thing that made sense was getting out of Sicily and far away from Lorenzo. She sucked in a breath and turned to face Lorenzo. When she spoke, she did so calmly and carefully. Much like she spoke to Gio when he was in the midst of a tantrum.

"Here's what we'll do, Lorenzo. I'll go home. You'll stay here. We'll make arrangements for you to meet Gio, of course. I'm not suggesting otherwise. But not when everything is so…up in the air." She didn't know why he was rattled by the press's knowledge, but she *did* want to keep whatever interest there was in Lorenzo away from her child. So it made no sense to bring Gio *here*. "I can't imagine why anyone would care all that much about a toddler, so we'll stay in New—"

"Dante will have planted a story to *make* people care." His gaze turned to hers, and she could not read it. It wasn't anger or even solely frustration. Something deeper and more complex sat there, making her ache for him when she should be angry with him. "I am afraid this changes things, Brianna. I cannot cave to your time line."

"Cave? My time line? Everything since you broke into my hotel room has been *your* idea, *your* time line."

He waved this away as if it was inconsequential, and she supposed it was. The current *consequences* were a business rival making an international story out of her son. Which didn't seem quite so serious as Lorenzo was making it out to be, not that she loved the idea. But Lorenzo was the expert on press and threats. Not her.

"Is he in danger?" Brianna forced herself to ask, even though she didn't know what recourse she had if he were. Just get home as fast as possible. "Are my parents?"

"I have dispatched every resource at my disposal to ensure everyone remains well protected. These reporters pose no direct threat to Gio or your parents, no. But I will be in charge of the public's access to my son so no threats can manifest."

Manifest. The idea of threats just *popping* up out of nowhere made her throat tight with fear. As if sensing this, something in his expression softened. In a move that shocked her, he took her hand in his.

"I will need you to trust me on this," he said earnestly. "But I will make you this vow—no harm will come to our son on my watch. He is my top priority. Always."

She had known a different man two years ago. A charming, passionate man with a certain amount of intensity for *certain* tasks. But not this. Not this sharp-edged, severe, heavy-handed pushing forward like an invading army.

And it was for her son. Her son's *safety* and *privacy.* So two years ago hardly mattered. The man she'd known, the woman she'd been. Her clattering nerves and old feelings that should be long gone didn't matter. Only getting to Gio and keeping him safe did.

So, when the car pulled to a stop and Lorenzo got out, Brianna followed. All the way back home to New Jersey.

Lorenzo spent much of the flight across the Atlantic on his phone. He had men on the ground in America, so he knew that no one had descended on Brianna's family just yet, and that he had people in place to stop them if they tried.

Perhaps Dante had been bluffing. Lorenzo mulled this over between phone calls, not allowing himself to look over at Brianna.

Last time he had, she'd been watching the dark night outside the plane's window. Her expression had been soft and sad and had made something turn and twist inside of him. The kind of twist that had caused him to break things off with her all that time ago.

A twinge that reminded him of a childhood torn by too many terrible things, all cemented by love and duty.

So he didn't look at Brianna. And when the plane landed and they were ushered off the plane, he kept his gaze forward, though he had to offer an arm. It seemed the right thing to do.

His assistant led them to the awaiting car, and then they began a long drive through darkness that was slowly headed toward dawn.

Brianna hadn't really slept, and it seemed to be catching up with her. Lorenzo only felt wired. Desperate to get his son away from any place he might be a target. Once they were back in Sicily, safely ensconced at his estate, he could breathe.

Until then…

The car eventually pulled into a very suburban area, full of modest but neat homes that all had the same sort of air to them. Cleanly manicured lawns, leafless trees in a nod to the windy cold. Brick two-stories. Not the kind of money he was used to these days, but definitely not the poverty he'd grown up in. Something firmly in the middle.

Their car pulled up at one of the older-looking homes and his assistant nodded back at him from his position in the front seat. Lorenzo looked over at Brianna, who had finally succumbed to sleep, her head against the window, her coat wrapped protectively around her like a bubble.

She'd changed in the bathroom when they'd gotten on the plane. Out of the beautiful sparkling gown and into a gray ensemble of what looked like some kind of athletic gear.

Lorenzo still wore his suit. It only dawned on him now that these were the clothes he would meet his son in. Hold his son for the first time in. He didn't know what would be the appropriate attire, but a suit hardly seemed it.

There was no time to alter it. Somehow, they had beat Dante's men here, or this had all been some kind of ploy. Either way, time was of the essence.

"Brianna."

She jerked awake, though he'd tried not to startle her. But she saw the house outside the window and was immediately shoving the door open. She sprinted through the yard and to the front door. Her purse dangled from her arm as she dug through it.

He arrived on the porch as she shoved keys into the door and turned the knob. She stepped inside the dimly lit entryway, and he followed.

He heard the sounds of people awake deeper in the house, though it was still well before 6 a.m. A woman who sounded a lot like Brianna said, "Mom's home!" and then the scrabble of little feet followed.

Lorenzo stood frozen by the door he'd closed behind him as a little boy bounded around the corner.

"Mama!" The boy shot across the floor and flung himself at Brianna as she crouched and caught him with ease. They held each other, just like that, for a very long time.

Lorenzo knew he should look at the two older people that had followed the boy into the room. Offer a handshake. A kind word. But he could only watch, mother and son wrapped up in each other. Love so evident he wished he didn't know. Wished he was blissfully ignorant of *this*.

"Baby, you shouldn't be up."

"I'm afraid he heard us making a bit of a racket trying to pack as instructed," the older woman said, fully dressed in slim slacks and a comfortable-looking sweatshirt.

Brianna stood, bringing Gio with her so the boy straddled her hip. Her blue eyes flickered with some emotion she hid well, although she was also clearly overjoyed at seeing her son again. "Gio. I want you to meet someone."

The boy turned his head to face Lorenzo. He had his short arms clutched around Brianna's neck, and when he looked at Lorenzo, tilted his head to lean it against Brianna's shoulder.

It was like being thrust back into time. Gio looked so much like his little brothers that Lorenzo felt as though he was that teenage boy once again, running herd on his younger siblings. With their dark shocks of hair and wild, expressive mouths. The only difference was the blue of Gio's eyes.

All Brianna.

"Gio," she said very softly. "This is your father."

The boy kept his head on Brianna's shoulder. He looked at Lorenzo with some speculation. Then he shook his head and turned away from Lorenzo, burying his face in the crook of Brianna's neck.

He mumbled something that sounded a lot like *scary.*

This seemed to amuse Brianna. "He is dressed a bit scary, isn't he?" she said with some humor and a nod at his dark suit. But her eyes were strangely wet. "But he isn't scary at all. I promise."

CHAPTER SIX

BRIANNA HAD NEVER seen Lorenzo quite so off his game. He had an arrested look on his face, and his eyes never left Gio. Like he was seeing the secrets to the world unfurl to him all at once—awe-inspiring and terrifying.

She supposed that was parenthood in a nutshell. And it made her want to cry—for so many reasons. Time lost. What clearly hadn't been a terrible decision in the first place considering they now had to secrete Gio away at some Sicilian estate. And the ache in her heart she couldn't fully get rid of, no matter how right she'd been to keep them apart.

Gio held on to her neck for dear life as he often did these days around strangers. Brianna's first instinct was to protect him. To say he didn't have to look at or talk to Lorenzo if he didn't want to.

But that was not how she dealt with anyone else connected to Gio. And that didn't do Gio any good. Though Lorenzo was essentially a stranger to him, the boy had to learn to be comfortable around his father.

She stepped closer to Lorenzo so he could get a better look at his son even if Gio was burrowed into her as tight as he could get. She wouldn't *force* him, but she would give him the space to get comfortable with his father.

"Gio," she said, holding him close so he didn't feel abandoned. "We're going to go on a trip."

Gio didn't loosen his grip, but he moved his head a little. "Zoo?"

"Not the zoo, sweetheart. We're going to go to a whole different country. You, me, Grandma, Grandpa and…your father." She tried to smile encouragingly at literally anyone in this room but wasn't sure she succeeded.

And she didn't know how to make an impromptu trip to Sicily sound exciting to a child who was just over a year old. She didn't know how to make any of this palatable to him.

"There are zoos I can take you to in Sicily," Lorenzo said, his voice oddly…soft. Maybe it wasn't so odd since he was talking to a child, *his* child. She'd just assumed someone like Lorenzo would have no clear idea of how to talk to a child. The people she knew who were never around children tended to be stiff and formal, and Lorenzo was often that in the best of times.

This was obviously not the best of times.

"Sicily, where we're going, is my home," he continued. He did not reach out to touch Gio, though she got the sense he wanted to. "So there are many places I can take you."

Gio didn't loosen his grip, but his gaze moved somewhat suspiciously to Lorenzo. "Roars?"

"That's his word for tiger," Brianna explained.

Lorenzo held the boy's suspicious gaze and smiled. A smile Brianna hadn't seen out of him since Florence. She did not like what that did to her defenses.

"Of course tigers."

A silence stretched out as Lorenzo and Gio surveyed each other, interrupted only when her father cleared his throat behind her.

Brianna turned to face him and tried to keep her smile in place. To treat her parents like she was treating Gio—timid toddlers who needed understanding and patience in a new situation.

"I'm sorry. Lorenzo, these are my parents. Scott and Helene. Mom, Dad, this is Lorenzo Parisi."

Lorenzo finally looked away from Gio and nodded at her parents, stepping forward and offering a hand. "It is good to meet you both."

Her parents each took a turn shaking the offered hand, and though they had polite smiles fixed on their faces, there was clear suspicion in both their expressions.

"I am delighted you will be accompanying us," Lorenzo said. "And apologize for the necessity of leaving on such short notice."

"We would do anything for our daughter and grandson," Mom said primly.

"Anything," Dad said, with an attempt at menac-

ing that might have worked on some football-playing boyfriend from high school, but hardly on this man.

Though Lorenzo nodded dutifully as if the threat had any weight against all his power and money.

"I've packed everything for Gio," Mom said. "We're almost done ourselves."

"Allow my staff to help you bring the bags to the car," Lorenzo said, gesturing for the door.

"We aren't ones for having people wait on us, Mr. Parisi."

"You must call me Lorenzo, and you must allow me to make this impromptu trip as easy on you and yours as possible."

Mom seemed to mull this over. "All right," she said eventually. "We'll finish packing." Her parents gave Brianna a look, but she could only smile over-brightly at them, hoping that at some point in the near future she'd be able to really talk with them.

But for now, it just… They had to go. She sucked in a breath as Lorenzo opened the door and gave instructions to his assistant and the driver who were to help with the bags.

"Do you have anything you need from here?" he asked, but his eyes were on Gio.

Brianna thought of her paints and embroidery supplies. It was the only thing of her own that she cared about. "I suppose not."

Lorenzo frowned. "There is no need to play martyr, Brianna."

She was too tired for her temper to flare. Mostly. "It's exhaustion, Lorenzo. Would I like my art supplies? Of course. Will my life look like something I can use art supplies in? How should I know? How could I possibly know what I need when I don't know what my life will look like in five minutes, let alone five days?"

She shifted Gio's weight, smoothed her hand over his flyaway dark hair. "But we'll have fun, baby," she said, forcing herself to sound cheerful. "An adventure!"

Gio didn't get excited about this, but he didn't voice his displeasure—which was a positive. He often voiced it and loudly.

But now there was only silence. The bustle of people going back and forth with bags. They were just waiting on her parents now, standing awkwardly in the entryway. Lorenzo never took his eyes off Gio, and Gio watched the man with careful wariness, never letting his grip on Brianna loosen.

"Would you like to hold him?" Brianna asked after a while. Because her back hurt, a migraine threatened, and if her parents didn't hurry up, she might actually go insane.

Lorenzo's smile was stiff and tight. Gio was practically strangling her—a clear sign he did not want to be held by a stranger. Brianna didn't *want* to hand him over to Lorenzo, but their first meeting should be more than this…surely.

"It is all right," Lorenzo said after a long while. "We will wait until he is ready. We have time."

We have time. It felt like a threat, even though it was only the truth. Who knew how long this would last? Who knew what lay ahead? All Brianna knew was she was doing this for Gio.

Everything was for Gio.

Safely on the plane, Lorenzo read the report from his head of security. They'd managed to waylay the small unit of journalists who'd been offered a tidy sum to get a picture of Brianna or her son, and they'd managed to make it back to the airport without detection.

A good start as they headed *back* across the ocean, this time with a toddler in tow. Lorenzo could not claim the flight was going *well*. Despite the attention of four adults determined to put every ounce of focus on Gio himself rather than dealing with each other, Gio did *not* enjoy the flight.

He screamed. He kicked. He ran about the cabin like some kind of wild, deranged beast. He hurled the remainder of his snack he didn't want and fought sleep like it was the very devil.

Lorenzo did not know why it filled him with a strange kind of pride.

Yes, be wild and untamable, son. Scream your displeasure. Get what you want. Always.

Brianna and her parents were clearly exhausted— both by the events of the day and Gio himself. The boy was tired and fighting it at every turn. The staff, used to children of all ages, were doing a pretty good job of keeping their feelings on the matter hidden behind stoic faces, but there were looks exchanged when the fever pitch of screams got especially high.

Like right now. Lorenzo got out of his seat and crossed to where Gio was huddled, ignoring his grandparents' attempts to calm him. Brianna sat in a seat like she'd given up. It was hard to blame her.

Lorenzo crouched in front of the boy, who immediately stopped screaming. His wide eyes studied Lorenzo in a mix of fear and uncertainty.

"Perhaps you'd like come with me to meet the pilot," Lorenzo offered pleasantly, holding out his hand though he didn't expect Gio to take it. It would take time for the child to trust him. "See how the plane is flown?"

On a whimper Gio scampered past him and to where Brianna sat, which was about what Lorenzo had expected. He didn't *want* his son to be afraid of him, but if he used that uneasiness to get Gio to sit still, the boy would no doubt drop.

Gio crawled up into the safety of Brianna's lap, shooting daggers out of his eyes at Lorenzo. But those eyes quickly began to droop now that he was forced to sit still. Just as Lorenzo had hoped.

Lorenzo crossed to the seat next to Brianna. Gio's eyes tracked him, blinking closed once, twice, and then finally staying there. His breathing evening out. His body relaxing in Brianna's arms.

Brianna relaxed, too, relief clear in her features. She even turned her head and smiled at him. "Good job," she whispered.

It should not fill him with warmth. That he'd succeeded. That Brianna had complimented him. Children at this age were easy enough to maneuver if you knew the tricks, and he'd had to learn them long ago.

It was a strange feeling, and one that made it easy not to be hurt by Gio's reticence, to be reminded of old responsibilities that had been thrust upon him too young. Responsibilities that had ripped his family into too many pieces. But he wasn't that powerless boy anymore.

He had *all* the power.

Which he was reminded of once again when they moved from plane to car, and then pulled up to his estate outside of Palermo. Saverina, his youngest sister, called it pretentious and over-the-top, while enjoying all its many amenities.

Lorenzo had been happy with both descriptors. The car pulled up the grand drive, around trees and fountains and marble fixtures that glittered in the sunlight. Brianna's parents practically had their noses pressed to the glass.

Lorenzo's staff stood waiting at the door. Everyone in the car filed outside and then the Andersen family simply stared, eyes wide and awed. No one seemed to know what to say. Even little Gio, who couldn't fully understand why this was impressive.

Lorenzo felt pride at this as well. Because *this* was the representation of his life's work. From hovel to *estate*. From hunger to *excess*. Luck might have played a role in just how far he'd climbed, but luck could only take a person so far.

"Come," he said. "We'll get you settled in."

No one spoke, but they followed him up the stairs

and into the grand entryway. Staff bustled by with bags and Lorenzo himself showed them to their quarters. An entire wing to themselves.

"I will leave you to rest. We will endeavor to begin a routine and stave off jet lag and serve dinner at seven. Should you need anything, there are phones in every room to contact staff. Feel free to explore in any ways you wish."

With that, he gave one last look at Gio…who was studying him intently. Lorenzo liked to believe there was less and less suspicion in the toddler's gaze, but it was hard to tell. Better he had some time with the family he knew in this unfamiliar place.

Lorenzo would be patient. Because they would never be separated again. He simply wouldn't allow it.

So he left Brianna and her family to settle in while he strode through the estate to the other wing. It would be in his best interest to rest, but he had to make certain there were no fires burning at Parisi Enterprises first. So he went to his office.

He lost track of time as he responded to emails and cleared his schedule for the next few days. There would be no leaving the estate until Gio began to look at him without fear, until he could figure out just what Dante was up to. So Lorenzo had to ensure all his seconds-in-command were ready to fill in for him.

He thought he heard something after getting off the phone, and when he looked up, Brianna stood in the doorway. Still in her casual travel wear, looking exhausted.

"Is there something you needed?"

She stepped into the room, studying the walls of bookshelves, the crystal chandeliers, the big windows that overlooked the beautiful grounds. She shook her head faintly, like she couldn't quite believe what was right in front of her.

"My mother informed me that I needed to thank you. She wouldn't stop harping on it, so I came to do that."

"Well, please, go on then."

She rolled her eyes. "I feel like I *should* thank you. The flights. Plural. This place. It's a lot, though clearly nothing you can't afford. Still...this whole thing is all your fault to begin with, so why should I thank you for it?"

Lorenzo's mouth firmed at that—though he wanted to scowl. "*All* my fault?"

"Yes." She moved through the room, looking at the spines of books, dragging her fingers across the back of a leather armchair in front of the broad fireplace that dominated one wall.

He should not find the casual ensemble or messy hair or tired eyes alluring, but he couldn't stop his eyes from taking a tour of her form. He had once known her body as well as his own. Perhaps they had only been together two months, but she had become something like a part of him.

That was the problem with Brianna. Among so many other things.

"So there's absolutely no blame on your own shoulders? For not telling me my son existed, that is."

She let out a long sigh. "Do you remember what you said to me when I said I wasn't going to beg for an apology for the way you broke things off with me?"

I'm not sorry.

But he didn't answer, because unfortunately he understood her point.

"I'm not sorry either, Lorenzo. I can't be. We've both done...what we felt needed to be done at the time. Now we've come together once again and our sole purpose is to protect Gio, correct?"

"Correct," he returned stiffly, because if they could remain on that same page, nothing bad needed to happen. No angry fights. No painful betrayals. Just a business partnership.

"Then, that's what we'll do. As...partners of sorts," she said, as if reading his mind. Then she turned to face him with those heartbreaking blue eyes. The color of the seascape above his mantel.

The one he'd bought *after* he'd broken things off with her, convincing himself it wasn't because of that shade of blue and her eyes.

"I hope very much you and Gio can have a real relationship," she continued, with that natural warmth that was simply a part of her. "One that keeps him safe and allows him a father. I don't want him to grow up without one."

She said nothing about what that meant for them.

Which was good because there was no *them*. Or shouldn't be.

But he was having a hard time thinking beyond the last time he'd seen her before these life-altering few days. Two years ago. Wrapped up in each other, pleasure and joy. A feeling so big, so dangerous, he'd slid out of bed the moment she'd fallen asleep. Packed his bags and left.

Because he would not love. He would not let such feelings tear him apart ever again. Not when he could help it.

And he could help it with her. Even if his body still ached for all they could bring out in each other. Lust and love got confused all the time. How well he knew this.

How well he kept them separate. And could. Always. Lust, he knew, gave him the upper hand, and didn't he need that now more than ever?

Something in the back of his mind whispered recriminations, arguments, warnings, but he could not heed them with his heart beating so loud. His body hard and wanting a taste.

Just a taste of what they'd once had. And why not? She was here. They were to keep *their* son safe. Together.

"There's just one problem," he said, moving from behind his desk to cross to her.

She watched him, wariness entering her expression the closer he got. But she did not back away. "What's that?" she asked, chin lifted. And it wasn't *all* wariness in those blue eyes.

She felt some echo of this as well. She had to.

He reached out and touched her cheek, just as he'd done the other night. Before he'd known. When he'd thought just another taste of her would solve the problem of Brianna. And maybe it was the sleep deprivation, but all he could think was he still hadn't had that taste.

Her breath caught, that flush creeping up her fair cheeks. So beautiful, his Brianna. *His*. He leaned close, and still she made no move to bolt, to stop him. He stopped when his lips were only a whisper away from hers. Then he met her gaze.

"You still want me."

CHAPTER SEVEN

THE WORDS SHOT through Brianna like flame itself. He need only look at her and she throbbed with a yearning she'd forgotten existed. Or tried to. But he was so close. The words…incendiary.

You still want me.

And *how*. But she did not just give in to wants these days. She had a son to think of, and she was so very exhausted, and oh, she missed kissing this man. The way he made it feel like the entire universe was only them. Only heat. Only that explosion of what he could make her body feel.

No one before him had ever come remotely as close. She hadn't even attempted to find *close* since. Even if there hadn't been a pregnancy, a son, she was certain he would have ruined her for all men. Forever.

You cannot be this weak.

"You're very conceited," she managed to say. Not forcefully exactly, but not as breathless as she felt. He was so close. She could see that dark ring of near-black around the outside of his brown eyes. Each individual whisker that shadowed his jaw after all the flying back and forth they'd done.

Had he slept? Had she? Was this real life or a dream? If it was a dream…surely she could indulge in a taste? She could lean forward, press her body to the strong wall of his. In a dream, she could relive everything she'd tried to forget.

His finger traced around her ear, then down her neck, and the sound she made was some embarrassingly desperate moaning sigh. Because his touch awakened every nerve ending, every foolish want she'd tried to tell herself not to have. He was going to crush her again. It was inevitable.

She didn't care. Not if he kissed her. She wouldn't care about anything.

Dimly, she knew this was stupid and ridiculous. A bad, bad move. But that throbbing inside of her had a mind of its own. Every millimeter of flesh felt sensitive. To air. To touch. To her clothes. Her breasts were heavy, and deep in the core of her she ached for something.

For him. Only him.

"You could walk away, Brianna. Leave this room. There is nothing holding you here, standing so close to me."

It felt like a lie. Like a million chains were holding her in place. Exhaustion, surely, allowing all that *want* to win. She knew better, and yet…

She did not leave. She did not put space between them. She could have and *should* have, just to prove to herself she could. But she didn't.

She swayed forward, this she knew. What she wasn't so sure about was who pressed their mouth to whose. Only that suddenly they were kissing—wild, hot, tinged with the pain they'd inflicted on each other, but this only made it a dark, potent emotion that took control.

Surely she had no control. Not when a fire like this could burn between two people. Simply by touching lips together. Lips then tongue, arms wrapped tight and bodies pressed together.

Two years seemed to vanish. *This* was everything she remembered. It didn't matter that her body had changed somewhat after pregnancy. Nothing between them had. His shoulders were still broad, his body hard, and the way he kissed her like she was a feast made just for him was every bit as intoxicating as it had been.

She arched against him, desperate for that friction that would bring her relief.

"Madness," he murmured, his mouth moving from her mouth to trail against her neck as his hand slid under the waistband of her pants. She might have thought to stop this if he hadn't said that. But if *he* thought it was madness, if *he* was too weak to fight it, then why should she be strong? Why shouldn't she embrace the madness?

Take it all the way.

His clever fingers found her core. She was nothing but sensation. But a desperate need to fall over that cliff he was running her toward. She moved with him as his mouth found her breast over her shirt.

Nibbled until she stiffened as the pulsing culmination swept through her.

Then he was pulling off her shirt and she was fumbling with the buttons of his pants.

Madness. Madness. Madness.

And she wanted it all. Here. Now. Nothing else mattered but this wild, whipping desire that even climax hadn't eradicated. She couldn't think past wanting him naked, on top of her, inside her.

It was wild, desperate. Like two people who had thought of little else in their two-year separation. And she might have understood that if it was just her pathetic self. But he seemed just as lost. Just as found. Just as desperate.

This "dangerous" billionaire who understood how to be patient with a toddler and how to protect a son.

Whatever warnings existed in her head were drowned out by him. His kiss. His touch. The harsh, hoarse way he said her name into her neck. Until she fell apart. The tantalizing words whispered in her ear as he laid her out on the warm, plush rug of his office.

Naked now. Him naked. He took a moment and simply stared at her as if taking her in, and it should have been a wake-up call. A moment of clarity.

But it wasn't. It never was with them.

He ran his hand down the center of her, between her breasts, over her stomach. A possessive move when she wasn't his. When he didn't *want* her to be. Because she would have been *anything* to him two years ago and he'd walked away.

Left her. Without a *word*. And she would simply... give in to him now? Without an apology? Without even a conversation of why he'd left things the way he had, or what he planned to do about it now? Just because it *felt* good?

No. She couldn't be that immature, that reckless.

She called on every last shred of control and determination the past two years had built inside of her and rolled out from under him. She didn't scramble. Because this wasn't about panic. It was about making the *right* choice.

It was about being the adult.

So they sat naked, ridiculously, on his plush office rug with the distance and cool air between them, their breathing more like panting in the now quiet room.

He said nothing. Which gave her the opportunity to take control of the situation and God knew she needed to be in control of *something*.

"I think we should chalk that up to some form of insanity brought about by lack of sleep," she said, even as she could barely catch her breath. Even as she wanted to give in to the heat in his gaze.

But she knew where that led. And it would be one thing to risk herself, her own heartbreak all over again. She thought if that was all there was, maybe she would have no choice but to follow this once more.

But she had Gio, and if she was heartbroken, she could hardly be strong enough to give him the father he deserved.

"I want you in my bed."

God, the way he growled that. She couldn't look at him or she'd be lost, so she calmly began to collect her clothes and worked on putting some censure in her tone. "Lorenzo."

"It is what you want too."

And how.

But she focused on the act of getting dressed. On the cold air around her now. On the truth of the situation.

The sex would be great. Life-altering—in more ways than one. But that was all it could be now. He'd had his chance for it to be more.

The chance was long gone.

"What I want? Physically? Sure. The sex would be good. It's always been good." Even that momentary lapse in her sanity had been *more* than good.

She didn't want to bare herself to him emotionally. Wanted to leave the nakedness and near miss of the situation as the only thing intimate between them.

But he had to understand. Maybe if he understood he would keep his distance. He would… They could be *partners* in this. Parenting.

Not sex.

So she forced herself to meet his gaze and spoke her truth. "But you…left me. You crushed me. I can't be crushed again. I have a son to protect. A mother doesn't get to follow her wants every which way. And I don't get the sense what happened here is about… anything more than chemistry."

If only. If only she didn't remember the afternoons

they'd spent in art galleries, hand in hand, arguing about different artists, the emotions different pieces should evoke. Elegant dinners where he'd spoken of the places he'd traveled, and she of the places she wanted to go. She had only realized in retrospect how cagey he had been about his own family, but she had told him everything about hers. And he'd asked questions. Remembered things.

He had been attentive. He had been *there*. And yes, there had been pockets of secrets. The kind of information he'd kept from her were the kinds of things that should have been a red flag, if she'd been more experienced, more worldly.

She should have known, yes. But in the moment she'd only been dazzled. That a man so handsome could find a not-so-special woman from New Jersey fascinating. That any man could listen, engage like he did. That they could be together as equals, *adults*.

He dressed carefully, saying nothing, until he stood there, a disheveled, gorgeous man with a frown on his face and the haze of lust in his eyes.

It hurt to look at him. To want him. Because one thing she knew for certain wouldn't change.

"What I want for myself is a real relationship," she said, forcing herself to maintain eye contact. "Built on love and respect and honesty. Not just for myself, but for Gio. I don't think you want that."

There was a strange beat of silence. He didn't look away. There was no guilt, no offense in his expression. Just a dark, unreadable intensity. "Love is a lie, *dusci*. A fairy tale. Love does not function in the real world."

She found it oddly comforting he thought so. Because he'd never said he'd loved her. So she'd never said it either, but she *had* loved him. So much it had scared her enough *not* to tell him.

But if he thought love was a lie, well, it was better than him just not loving *her*.

Maybe? God, she needed some rest. First she had to extricate herself from this without compounding a mistake. "I don't agree, but I don't need to. What I need is to make certain we're on the same page. We can co-parent. Hopefully as friends. What I cannot do is engage in this sort of behavior that threatens to put us at odds. We have to be on the same page for Gio, as much as possible. Having sex complicates things." She sucked in a fortifying breath. "We can't muddy the waters with a physical relationship. So we'll agree to work together to parent Gio, to determine how that works with our individual lives and his protection and safety. For our son. And everything from before…and this little blip… Well, we'll leave that behind. Do you agree to these terms?"

He was very still and very intently staring at her for a minute or so, then nodded. He even held out his hand, like they were shaking on some business partnership. She supposed, in a way, they were.

She moved forward, took his hand and shook it. Very professionally, she liked to think. But as she moved to pull her hand back, he held tight.

"We will indeed parent Gio together, come to a

mutually beneficial conclusion as to what a future looks like with us both in his life," he said.

Her heart was tripping over itself, though she couldn't say why. Just because he was holding her in place? Just because the brown of his eyes seemed dark and endless. Just because her body still throbbed and yearned for more—specifically *him*, deep inside her.

"And while we do that, you may remain as distant as you wish. I will not pursue you. I will not seduce you. But I will not pretend, Brianna. When I want you. When I'm thinking about how you feel under my hands, how you sound when I am deep within you."

She let out a shuddering breath. *Oh, dear.*

His grip on her hand tightened and he drew her near, his mouth dipping close to her ear. "And I will not say no should you come begging to finish what we've started," he said, his voice a low scrape close to a whisper but not quite.

Not quite.

Luckily the idea of begging gave her just a shred of backbone in the moment. She jerked her hand out of his. She tried to tell him it'd be a cold day in hell, but her mouth wouldn't form the words. Or her conscience wouldn't let her say them. All she managed was a very ineffective "Fine."

And then she scurried away like prey escaping a predator. Because that was *exactly* what she felt like.

CHAPTER EIGHT

LORENZO WATCHED HER leave his office. She hurried. She looked back once over her shoulder. Much like when he'd first seen her again at the art gallery. But instead of fear this time, there was something else.

She wasn't running away from *him*. She was running away from what her body *wanted* from him.

He quite enjoyed that.

But once he turned back to his office and tried to remember what he'd been doing, what needed to be done, he was met only with his brain reliving that moment her mouth had touched his again.

Two years. It should have erased this grasping, painful thing inside of him. The kind of *thing* that tore people apart. That destroyed them…or worse, gave a person the tools to destroy themselves.

He could admit, now that he was alone and had a few moments to collect himself, that this had been… ill-advised. At best.

He did not relish having lost his control, or her being the one to find it first. It was an affront to acknowledge that his sharp mind had been lost to the taste of her and the feel of her and the noises she made as he made her fall apart in his arms.

I think we should chalk that up to some form of insanity brought about by lack of sleep.

He grunted irritably. She was not *wrong*, and this was why he'd said that last bit. He'd needed to get a shot in too. She could claim it was about Gio, but it was about *them*.

You crushed me.

Two years ago, he had given no thought to what she might feel. Not really. Oh, he'd known she'd be hurt. He knew she fancied herself in love with him and was just waiting for him to say it first.

He'd known all of that. But leaving had been an act of survival. Self-protection. He'd been more worried about getting *himself* out than what the aftermath might be for *her*.

Even now, he hesitated to put himself in her shoes. He could not be sorry for what he'd done. It was the only course of action he'd seen then. Now.

What might have happened if he'd stayed? If they'd found out about Gio's existence together?

You would have been there from Gio's first breath. You would have torn the world apart.

He did not particularly care for that much clarity or insight into himself. Into the man he'd been two years ago. He would have handled it—Brianna, a child.

But he would have done it badly. Two years ago, Saverina had only just gone off to university in England—her dream, and with his youngest sibling out of his house, it had been the first time he'd had the time or space not to be the 24-7 father figure in his siblings' lives. A child would have been...

Why was he thinking about this? It did not matter. He *hadn't* known. Brianna had kept Gio from him. He didn't need to hold on to his anger over that—it was hard to when he understood her motivations were about protecting Gio. What he needed to do *now* was figure out how to move forward.

His people were still outmaneuvering Dante when it came to press coverage. So far, only a few piddly gossip sites had picked up the story and only the most die-hard of gossipmongers cared.

It would spread. You couldn't shove a story back into a bottle once it escaped, but he would have the time to craft *his* version of what that story would be. Dante wanted to paint him the villain. The deserter.

This wouldn't work for a wide variety of reasons. But Lorenzo had to have a good story in place as counterpoint. Irrefutable counterpoint.

He could marry Brianna. He ignored the spurt of something that went through him—an emotion that would do no one any good, so best not identified or labeled.

There was no good story to excuse away the two-year discrepancy between pregnancy and a union. Besides, this was a rather traditional way of thinking—marry the mother of your child. Dante and Marino Industries were traditional. Old money. Royal ties.

Lorenzo had always known he couldn't compete

with that. So he'd fashioned himself a start-up. Sleek. Modern. The violence accusations had been a hit, but knowledge of a secret son would not be unless he pretended he was as traditional as Dante and this hidden son was a blight, a *bastard,* rather than a gift.

Instead, Lorenzo would create a modern story. He would use the truth and paint Dante and his unfounded accusations the villain that had kept him from his son. He and Brianna had parted amicably. And now, like so many others in his position, they would co-parent. Reasonable, responsible adults who had engaged in a short affair and were now fond of each other, but definitely not meant for something like marriage.

Though it wouldn't work if they both remained single. There would be too much room for a variety of gossip. No, he would need to get the ball rolling on finding someone else to marry. To create the perfect image of blended family.

Dante Marino's counterpoint. Always.

Lorenzo's potential wife would need to be someone who fit his vision for a modern billionaire. Definitely not an *American*. Ideally, someone with traditional ties he could use for Parisi Enterprises, but who knew how to work the press. Maybe someone in publicity. He would have his assistant create him a potential list.

He would not think of Brianna whispering his name while he'd touched her.

If he kept everything about business, love would never muddy the waters.

He sent a few missives off to staff and then, noting it was almost time for dinner, changed gears. He would find a way to win the press wars with Dante, but here at home, in private, he needed to win over his son.

He went to his wing. Stefano had two little ones, so Lorenzo had made sure the estate was outfitted for them whenever Stefano came to visit. It made Lorenzo an uncle, not a grandfather, and considering Stefano was only a few years younger than him it was hardly unorthodox. Still those two little hellions made Lorenzo feel *old*.

He bypassed this feeling by going to a bin of toys, fishing out the plastic creature he knew to be buried in there, and then returned downstairs. As he headed toward the dining room, he heard the soft sounds of voices—no doubt Brianna and her family.

He came around a corner, coming face-to-face with the quartet. Gio, who had been running forward, came to a skidding halt right at his feet. Slowly, the boy looked up and up, like he'd just run into a monster in a horror movie.

Lorenzo crouched and held the plastic tiger between them. "This was my brother's," he offered without preamble. "Perhaps you'd like to play with it during dinner."

Gio studied the tiger. He looked back at his mother, then at Lorenzo. He grabbed the tiger, then quickly retreated behind Brianna's legs.

She reached down and stroked his dark hair. "Gio. What do you say?"

The boy peered at him from safety behind Brianna, but he was clutching the tiger. "Tank you," the little boy muttered, not making eye contact. Though he darted little glances Lorenzo's way as they headed into the dining room and then all throughout dinner, while he played with the tiger in between Brianna's urgings to him to eat.

This gave Lorenzo a deep satisfaction. As did slowly winning over Brianna's parents until they relaxed rather than looking around the opulent room suspiciously. Even Brianna looked somewhat relaxed.

"Brianna was telling us that one of the art shows she was meant to attend originally is tomorrow night. She's saying she's going to skip it, and we both think she should go," Brianna's father said, watching Lorenzo speculatively. "What do you think?"

"Of course she should go." He turned his attention from Scott to Brianna. "You will all have a car at your disposal. If you need anything, you need only ask Maria. She will be your personal assistant while you're here. I'm afraid I must insist on a bit of a security detail to make certain the press won't become a problem, but there's no reason for you to miss it."

"I think we'd feel better if you went with her," Helene said earnestly.

Lorenzo hadn't expected *that*. He'd expected their continued distrust, figured this was some kind of a test. He cleared his throat. Going with Brianna would pose a problem with his current plans.

"I am right here," Brianna said, wiping Gio's

messy mouth with a napkin. "And can make all these arrangements and decisions on my own."

"But you won't," her father grumbled, lifting his glass to take a sip.

"Lorenzo does not need to play chaperone. I've handled this before and can handle it again."

"But that was before…" Helene trailed off and glanced at Lorenzo. A clear look that said, *This is all your fault, so you should clean up the mess.* "Before the tabloids took an interest."

Lorenzo didn't say anything at first, and Brianna didn't look at him. She very carefully and purposefully kept all her attention focused on Gio.

"Done. Done!" The boy started shouting when Brianna tried to urge him to take another bite. He flung out his arms, and would have toppled his cup if Scott hadn't been quick to pluck it out of the way. As Lorenzo watched the three of them working as a team with such ease, something sharp and painful lodged in his chest.

"He's tired," Brianna said. "He needs a bath and a good night's sleep. You all stay and finish your dinners. Say good night, Gio."

Before the boy could say anything, Lorenzo stood. "I will come with you."

"You don't—"

"I would like to be a part of as many routines as possible. Both so he gets used to having me around, and so I understand what needs should be met."

Brianna opened her mouth, like she was going to argue, but in the end she only shut it and nodded.

She lifted Gio onto her hip, encouraged him to give his grandparents a good-night hug, then they exited the dining room together.

"Roar bath?" the boy said, holding up the toy Lorenzo had given him before dinner.

"Yes, the tiger can come in the bath with you," Brianna said, following Lorenzo up the stairs to the wing he'd put her family in.

Lorenzo unlocked the built-in baby gate and opened it to let Brianna through.

"Was this left over from a previous owner? It's very helpful."

"No, I had it installed a few years ago for my niece."

"I guess that's a billionaire's prerogative, isn't it?" She moved down to their rooms and flipped on the light in the room he'd assigned her. It connected to the nursery, so she could either close the door and have privacy and use the monitors or leave the door open and feel as though they were in the same room together.

She moved for a suitcase, then turned to Lorenzo, who stood in the doorway. "What should he call you?"

"Call me?"

"Dad? Daddy? Father? A Sicilian word you'd prefer?"

Lorenzo blinked. In all of this, learning and accepting he had a son, meeting him, working to win him over, this was a strange thing not to have thought of. But it had not occurred to him that this little boy would have a word *for* him. His niece and nephew called him Zu. His brothers and sisters called him by name.

And it had been so many years since his father's death that he hadn't thought of how to address a father in so very long.

Pá.

No, he did not want to think of his father. Did not want that association. That bitterness when he heard his own son call out to him. He would never betray his son the way his own father had.

"Why don't we keep it simple?" Brianna said gently, as if she sensed that he was lost. At sea. "He calls me Mama, so we'll go with Dada. Gio, can you go to Dada for a second?"

Gio shook his head furiously and tightened his grip on Brianna. She sighed. "I need to put you down so I can get your clothes. Do you want to pick out your pajamas?"

This time he nodded. Brianna put him on the ground and he clutched her hand, sending those suspicious looks back at Lorenzo.

Lorenzo had been determined not to let it hurt. The child hadn't known of a father's existence all this time, and couldn't be expected to accept Lorenzo in a single day. Lorenzo understood that these were vulnerable years for children. Best that the boy be suspicious and careful. Much better than the alternative.

But Lorenzo already loved his son with a depth that threatened to split him open and no matter how rational it was for the boy to not trust him, it continued to shove a little shiv of pain under his heart.

Love was the enemy, yes, but he would always protect his own. Never let love leave him weak and vulnerable again. When he took care, protected, it was okay. He did not allow anyone else to risk, to sacrifice. That was his job, and it always would be.

It was why Brianna and Gio were here. It was why he would send a security detail with Brianna to the art show. He would build a life for them here where they were all safe and taken care of. Part of a careful compartment of his life that did not…complicate things.

Gio picked out his pajamas and Lorenzo led Brianna to the bathroom well equipped for a child's bath. He gathered the necessities, including the little bath toy set his niece used. He ran the water, tested the temperature. When he turned to Brianna she was watching him with open-mouthed shock.

"*How*…do you know how to do all this?"

He didn't want to tell her. Not because it was some great secret, but because…he was very careful. Not to expose pieces of himself that she might use against him. Twist to make him something he couldn't be.

But perhaps if she understood, she would trust him alone with Gio sooner rather than later.

"I have brothers and sisters, and I am the oldest and had to help take care of them quite a bit."

"How many?"

A tricky question he also didn't want to answer. She could find the information out there on the in-

ternet, no doubt. Though not all of it. The depth of
the horrible story that was Rocca. Only that he had
once been the oldest of ten, and now he was the oldest of nine.

But he could never bring himself to lie, to pretend
like Rocca did not exist. It felt too wrong. "There
are eight now."

"Why *now*?" Brianna asked, carefully undress-
ing the wriggling Gio who was clearly eager to play
with the bath toys in the large bath.

My twin sister died because love is poison.

But he wasn't going to say *that*.

"Unfortunately, Rocca passed away a few years
ago."

"Oh, Lorenzo." Brianna looked up at him, that
easy warmth that radiated from her making the empathy seem less like the dreaded *pity*, and more like
something akin to comfort. "I'm so sorry. I don't
know what it's like to have siblings, but that must
have been terrible. What happened?"

"It is of no matter. She is gone." A waste of a life
all because their father was a spineless coward, and
their mother was lost to love. Broken, so broken,
and he had learned you could not put broken things
back together.

Brianna did not press. She picked up Gio and
placed him in the bath. She knelt next to it as she
soothed his whining resistance at getting his hair
shampooed.

When Lorenzo knelt next to her, she sent him a

speculative look but offered no recriminations. She just handed him the washcloth so that he could help.

They washed the boy, let him play. It was very domestic and reminded him of days long gone. Those quiet moments with his brothers and sisters when he'd thought he and Rocca could protect them from everything. That they were better than their parents.

And then Rocca…

He would not go back to that place. Those feelings. He was in the present now. Money at his disposal. The remainder of his siblings safe and sound, with all they could ever want at their fingertips.

And he was kneeling here at the bath, hip to hip with Brianna. She was sunlight and warmth, and *that* was more dangerous than memories. She would be his end if he gave in to this feeling that was once again roiling about his chest, just as it had two years ago. As if he'd learned nothing.

Gio's hand slapping against the water sending a spray of water up and out of the tub was a welcome distraction from said feeling, and Lorenzo laughed at the boy's exuberance while Brianna gently scolded him.

But, sensing an ally, Gio splashed again, looking at Lorenzo for another laugh. Lorenzo gave it, because he would give anything to have his son look at him without suspicion.

Gio splashed with wild abandon now. And Brianna, droplets of water cascading down her hair and her face, glared at him. "If you're such an expert on children, you should know better than to laugh at such behavior."

"Ah, but my son should have all the fun he wants."

"He'll be spoiled in that case."

"I do not see anything wrong with that. I have worked hard. Why not allow my son everything that I did not have?"

Her eyes were so very blue and warm when she turned them on him. "What did you not have?"

He shrugged and looked back at Gio, who would no doubt have the tub well rid of water by the time he was done. "If you searched my name when you found out you were pregnant, you know I built myself and my empire from nothing. That is no exaggeration. We were very poor."

"With so many children," Brianna said, that same, soft empathy in her voice so that it didn't rankle as it did when other people spoke of it. "I can't say I grew up like this, but I never worried about money. I suppose as the only child I was spoiled after a fashion." She looked at Gio, and he could not begin to guess what she was thinking, as she said nothing else.

She informed Gio it was time to get out—which the boy *loudly* argued against—but they worked together to dry him off and get him dressed, both a little soaked themselves.

Brianna carried him back to the bedroom and Lorenzo followed. Since Brianna offered no objection, he walked through her room to the adjoining children's room. Watched as she laid Gio down, handed him a frayed-looking bear. She sang him a very short little song and his eyes drooped immediately.

She motioned Lorenzo to follow her, carefully and quietly back to the open doorway to the adjoining room.

"He's getting brave enough to try to climb out, so I'll leave the main door closed and the one between us open. No one will leave the gate open, will they?" she said in a low voice that wouldn't wake the child.

"Of course not. I'll have the toddler bed moved into this room tomorrow if that would make you more comfortable."

"A toddler bed. For your niece?"

"Yes."

"With so many brothers and sisters, are you overrun with nieces and nephews?"

"Not just yet. Many of my siblings are much younger. Saverina is only now twenty, but Stefano is only two years younger than I. He works for me at my offices in Rome, so sometimes business dictates he visit Palermo, and he likes to bring his family. As well he should."

They fell into a comfortable silence, standing there and watching the easy rise and fall of their son's chest in the dim light.

"I feel like I should apologize for my parents," she said quietly. "You don't have to go to the art show with me. I'm quite certain I can handle it."

"I would feel better having my eye on you, but it's best if we're not photographed together again until

I can fully curate the story I wish to reveal. Perhaps this could work if I brought a date."

"A date?"

When he looked down at her, confused by the sharp note in her voice, he saw eyebrows furrowed and mouth curved in a frown.

"Yes. So there's no speculation about *us*. We'll make it clear we aren't together."

"We *just* had…" She dropped her already quiet voice to a complete whisper. "Practically had sex. Like a few hours ago. And you're going to go…date someone tomorrow night?"

"Practically doesn't count, Brianna. But yes. You made it quite clear you did not want to engage in any kind of relationship."

"No, Lorenzo, *you* made that clear."

It was his turn to frown at her. "This has nothing to do with…feelings."

"Maybe for you, but I still *have* feelings, Lorenzo. I don't have to like them for them to exist."

"What exactly are they?"

She seemed arrested by the question, and he should be arrested by it as well. He never should have asked it. He shouldn't be *here*. Gio was asleep. Nothing more was needed of him until morning.

"What do you remember about our time together?" she asked him. He didn't have the first clue why she'd ask him that in this conversation, but the answer was in his head even though he didn't want it.

Everything.

Walks under the stars where she'd told him about

her art, what inspired her, what she hoped to do. What the summer in Florence meant to her.

She had been so full of hope and light. Everything he knew of becoming successful was grit and hard work and sacrifice. The strangling balance between ensuring all his brothers and sisters had everything, while also building an empire that would see them always well looked after.

That trip to Florence had been the first thing he'd ever done for himself and only himself, and Brianna had been the fresh air he'd desperately needed. The idea that on the other side of this moment there could be such sparkling optimism.

And then she'd started to look at him with something deeper in her eyes than the dazzlement he'd seen when they first met. Like she knew him, though he never spoke of his past. Like she could offer him this brand-new world and he could be in it. They could be in it. Together.

And he had remembered. What it felt like to hope. What it felt like to think he'd finally arrived at a place where he could relax.

And Rocca's cold, lifeless body. A victim to all that hope.

"Lorenzo—"

But he did not wish to go back to Rocca's death. To his summer with Brianna. You could not go back. You could only go forward. "If you do not wish me to be there, I do not need to be."

She sighed and rolled her eyes, as if he was the

biggest fool she'd ever met. "Good night, Lorenzo," she said, pointing him toward the door.

And though he was not one for obeying orders, he left. Because it was better than staying and risking everything.

CHAPTER NINE

BRIANNA SLEPT LIKE the dead. Luckily, no amount of inner turmoil had been able to stop the complete and utter exhaustion that had claimed her. When she woke up, groggy and unsure of where she was, she still felt like she'd been hit by a truck, but at least like she could handle the damage of all that.

The truck that was Lorenzo and this place and her life upended. She could handle it because she had to. For Gio.

She didn't hear him making any noise in his crib, so she didn't get out of bed. But when she grabbed her phone, she saw a text from her parents.

Heard G babbling as we went down to breakfast. Took him with us.

At the mention of breakfast, Brianna realized she was starving. She should get dressed and head downstairs. Take Gio off her parents' hands. But the bed was so soft, the quiet so nice, and all her inner agitation from yesterday was still *right* there.

She'd almost had sex with Lorenzo. Just…right there in his office, like she had no will power whatsoever. She could blame it on fatigue or any number of things, but it didn't change the fact that she'd allowed far too much, even if not that final act.

Worse, enjoyed it.

She could not repeat it if she had any sense of self-preservation at all, even though a repeat seemed to be all she could consider.

I will not say no should you come begging.

She let out a shuddering breath, too many sensual memories assaulting her. Yesterday. Two years ago. She did not understand how two bodies could be so clearly made for one another, but their minds and hearts could be on such different planets.

Well, they agreed on Gio. They agreed on hard work and art. They had always had plenty to talk about *before*, so it wasn't like they weren't well suited.

But she believed in love.

And he thought it was a fairy tale.

A man who took care of his little brothers and sisters, and then their children. Who installed toddler gates and had beds and cribs and playrooms. Who knew how to bathe a child, how to be patient with them. How to accept them so easily, so wholly.

The two things did not compute for her. He loved his family deeply. Protected them, provided for them, clearly, if his brother with children worked for him. He was a *family* man.

And he did not believe in love. She couldn't work

it out in her mind. Everything about her small family was centered in love.

She thought of the way he'd talked about his sister, the one who'd died. She'd thought if he really didn't want to discuss it, he wouldn't have mentioned her at all. But he'd gone completely blank when he'd said, *It is of no matter. She is gone.*

Gone.

Maybe there was more to that story. Or maybe there was another story. A lost love before her. Something that had soured him on the idea of *romantic* love, and so he threw all that he had inside of him into those he was related to.

Which she was still trying to wrap her mind around, since she hadn't known he was from such a large family. When she'd been searching for information about him after finding out about Gio, she hadn't seen much beyond business articles and the screaming stories about his violent tendencies and ruthless tactics that had left his rival's son in a hospital bed.

Nothing about *nine* siblings. Nothing about a sister who'd passed. Nothing about who he'd been before he'd become Parisi Enterprises.

Brianna contemplated the phone in her hand. She knew more now. Details that might allow her to find out about his family. It would be wrong to do an internet search on the sister he'd lost. Wrong to poke into his private life that way. An invasion of privacy. And who knew if the information would even be correct. She was quickly learning gossip columns didn't need a shred of truth or evidence to print whatever might get clicks or sell magazines.

But did she owe Lorenzo scruples when he had essentially put Gio in danger by allowing knowledge of him to be leaked to his rival?

Or was that your own fault for coming to Palermo at all?

Brianna blew out a breath. Maybe it wasn't about fault. Maybe it was just that…choices had consequences. Unforeseen ones. And a person had to deal with them without worrying about whose fault those consequences were.

And with that thought, she set her phone aside and got ready for the day. She wanted to spend it with Gio, because she'd be going to the art show tonight. She tried not to think about how much she hated the idea of Lorenzo attending with a date.

He could do whatever he wanted with whomever he wanted. He did not want any kind of serious relationship and she couldn't engage in anything else, not with Gio involved. It was all very mature and adult, really. He *should* date. Touch whomever he wanted. Have sex with a hundred women on his office floor.

She accidentally snapped the hair band in her hand by pulling it too hard. The sting of the snap was enough to remind her that what she'd said to him last night was true and perfectly acceptable.

She didn't have to *like* her feelings to have them. The truth was, no matter how pathetic, she hadn't fully gotten over Lorenzo in their two years apart.

She'd been able to set aside her broken heart while focusing on becoming a mother, but it didn't change the fact that accepting he wasn't a violent threat to Gio meant…he was just the man she'd known.

Loved.

And how did she just get over that? Never had she felt such a connection to a man before, and maybe that was one-sided. Maybe his escape was simply growing tired of her and not wanting to deal with the fallout.

But if he didn't believe in *love*, maybe his sudden, unexplained exit two years ago had been less about her not mattering at *all*, and more about her mattering…a great deal.

She paused with the hairbrush halfway through a stroke in her hair. If she hadn't mattered, he wouldn't have *escaped* like a scared man. Wouldn't he have just told her it was over? Wouldn't it have all happened at a normal hour? Not sneaking away in the middle of the night like a desperate man.

Brianna sat with this thought for a while, not knowing what to do with it. If she'd had it back home, before she'd reunited with him, she would have told herself she was a fanciful idiot.

But every way he'd behaved toward Gio, every new thing she learned about him in these short few days…did not speak to a man who ran away. Something had to *prompt* the escape.

Could it have been fear?

She rolled her eyes at herself. Now she was really grasping for straws. She finished getting ready and then went downstairs in search of her parents and son. They weren't in the dining room, but the staff insisted she sit and eat something, and since she was hungry, she didn't argue.

She ate and drank some coffee and texted her parents. They texted back they were in the playroom upstairs, so once she was done Brianna went to find them.

When she did, she realized it wasn't just her parents and Gio, it was Lorenzo as well. Gio had a little bin of brightly colored plastic balls in one corner, and Lorenzo was sprawled on the floor in the other. They were clearly engaging in some game. Gio never got too close, but he threw balls Lorenzo's way and squealed in delight every time Lorenzo made an exaggerated effort to catch the ball, and then dramatically bobbled it before catching it securely.

Her parents sat on a little couch, clutching mugs of tea, smiling indulgently at both of them. Brianna stood in the doorway, watching silently, her heart swelling painfully in her chest.

This was everything Gio deserved. And Lorenzo too. He was obviously a man born to be a father, or perhaps made to be one through circumstance. But clearly, any child was lucky to have Lorenzo in their corner.

She got a little choked up about it, but she didn't let herself cry. Just watched her son and his father engage in their little game and tried not to hope too hard for anything more than this perfect moment.

* * *

Lorenzo was playing with his son. He didn't let himself dwell on it too deeply. Later, in private, he would allow himself to feel the full joy of this moment, but for now he simply juggled another ball and watched Gio's face light up in delight.

He knew Brianna's parents were watching because they didn't fully trust him yet, but he could feel their approval. This would be important—Gio clearly loved them as much as they doted on their grandson.

Lorenzo didn't allow himself to think about introducing his siblings to his son, about bringing Gio into the Parisi fold. If he did… Well, all these emotions threatened to make him foolish. When he needed a clear head to ensure his son was protected.

He wasn't sure exactly what caught his attention—had she made a noise? Had that subtle scent reached across the room and teased him? Was there something elemental about them—a magnetism that meant he would always know when she was near?

But he glanced over and Brianna stood in the doorway. She was watching the game, her eyes shiny, though she wasn't crying. And it was not sadness on her face, but joy. A joy that echoed inside of him, bright and warm, like the time they'd been together before.

He was going to have to find a better way to navigate this. It was too dangerous. *She* was too dangerous.

Lorenzo must have looked too long in her direction, because Gio turned his attention to the door. He immediately forgot the balls and scrambled over to his mother, happily yelling, "Mama!" the whole way.

She knelt down to accept his eager hug and squeezed him tight. Just like when she'd greeted him at the house in New Jersey. As if they'd been parted for a long time when it couldn't have been more than twelve hours.

"Are you having fun?" Brianna asked, smiling as she brushed Gio's flyaway hair back.

Gio held up a red ball in Brianna's face. "Ball!" Then he flung it Lorenzo's way.

Lorenzo felt a bit foolish doing it in front of Brianna, God knew why, but he engaged in the same exaggerated bobbling before securing the ball.

Gio laughed hysterically as Brianna hitched him onto her hip. Before she could say anything, her parents stood.

"We're going to go take a walk around the gardens. It's supposed to be a lovely day and we could use some fresh air."

"We'll go with," Brianna said. "I'm sure Gio's ready to run around a bit."

But Brianna's mother stopped her before she could follow. "He's having fun here, Bri," she said gently. "Meet us there in a bit."

Brianna glanced back at Lorenzo, then nodded at her mother. Once her parents had left, Lorenzo and Brianna stood in the playroom in an uncomfortable silence.

"You have wonderful parents," Lorenzo said, hating that his voice sounded gruff. But he appreciated everything the Andersens had been so far. Stability for their grandson. A rock for their daughter. Kind to him when they didn't have to be, even if he was housing them at the moment.

But this wasn't about debts. This was about giving Gio and Lorenzo the opportunity to be together as father and son. And not every parent would have been as gracious as hers.

"I do. I'm very lucky." Brianna brushed her hand over Gio's hair again. "You don't speak of your parents," she said keeping her gaze on their son.

Lorenzo found it difficult to say the words even though the wound was old now and shouldn't hurt quite so much. "Dead."

Brianna said nothing to that, but she nodded. She kept her gaze on Gio. "Can Dada hold you for a minute?"

Gio looked at Lorenzo. Lorenzo smiled, but he did not hold out his arms. He wouldn't pressure the child. But something about the game or the sleep must have softened little Gio's heart somewhat. He reached out a hand. Half-heartedly and a little uncertainly, without giving Brianna any verbal yes.

But it was enough. Lorenzo felt his heart clatter against his chest, like he was a young man making a business presentation for the first time, certain everyone in the room could read the *poor* on him.

But he'd succeeded then and he knew how to hold a child. He reached out and took Gio's willing form. Gio didn't wrap his arms around Lorenzo like he did when Brianna held him, but he sat there without reaching back for Brianna or giving Lorenzo a suspicious look. He paid attention to the ball in his hand.

Lorenzo felt frozen. He was holding his son. In his arms. The boy played with the ball, slapping it against Lorenzo's free hand. Lorenzo simply looked down at Gio for the longest time, trying to memorize the weight of him. The shape of his nose. Those blue eyes on the otherwise very *Parisi* face.

Lorenzo swallowed, trying to find his balance. Without thinking it through, he looked to Brianna, as if she could give to him that balance he so desperately needed. But she was watching with her hands clasped, a bright smile on her face even as a tear trickled down her cheek. She wiped it away before Gio saw.

Lorenzo wanted to reach out. Bring her into this perfect circle. So that they could be a family. So that this could be his life. These days, he got whatever he wanted, so why not this? Why not make *this* everything it could be?

But he did not move. Because he knew the dangerous feeling that swelled inside of him when Brianna was near. Then or now it did not matter. What he felt for her was too big, too complicated, and far too threatening.

Family only worked when one person was in charge. When one person was beholden only to the responsibilities of taking care of a family.

Being in love led to inequality. Weakness. It twisted things. Took the focus off the children and protecting them and put it on desperate needs that could only ever destroy everything.

So he held his son and did not reach out for Brianna. Did not attempt to bring her into this moment.

He focused on Gio. His son.

Not the woman who had stolen his heart long ago. Let her have it. Let her keep it. He had no need for it anyway.

CHAPTER TEN

BRIANNA DID NOT let herself break down in front of Gio. She waited. She got through the day until she could excuse herself to go get ready for the art show.

Then she let herself cry. Sob, really. Just let all the swirling emotion out. It felt so wrong that Lorenzo and Gio had lived without each other for over a year. All because of another man's lies and her own fears.

And the worst part was this overwhelming emotion wasn't *just* about the time lost. The beauty of father and son together. It was more than that.

How was she supposed to endure this and not feel all those old, loving feelings? Lorenzo was the same man she'd known. Little had changed. Except she was getting more and more glimpses into what he'd come from, and that only made him more understandable. More wonderful.

His parents were dead. His sister too. Lorenzo had taken care of the rest of them, clearly, all while building his own empire. She had no doubt he'd accomplished said empire *because* of everything he'd had to take care of.

She wasn't sure how he'd accomplished it all. It was awe-inspiring.

She supposed his siblings might have another view of him, but if his brother visited with his children often enough for Lorenzo to have outfitted his house for them, surely they were close.

And it would mean Gio had cousins. Aunts and uncles. A much larger family than the one he'd known. The kind of thing Brianna herself had always dreamed of but not been able to create for Gio herself.

She knew she should want to go back to her life in New Jersey once it was safe. Find normalcy once again. But she just…didn't. She wanted to stay here. With Lorenzo. With a whole big world and family to give to her son. She wanted Lorenzo holding Gio to become so normal it didn't make her want to sob alone in her room.

She wanted all of that for Gio, but she worried if that was because she also wanted it—and Lorenzo— for herself. She pondered that. Was this really selfish? Did she care more about her own wants and desires and what had happened in Lorenzo's office than what was best for her son? Was she just convincing herself it was all for Gio?

She sat with that worry for a moment, but she couldn't latch on to it. Gio deserved a good father and Lorenzo fit the bill. If Lorenzo's siblings were half as good with children as Lorenzo himself, that was more love and care for Gio than she had even imagined for him.

Maybe she yearned for those things too, but it wasn't at the expense of her son. So there was that. But there was also the lure of Lorenzo.

A headache threatened, so she focused on getting ready rather than the man causing it. She got dressed. Did her own hair and makeup though Lorenzo's staff had offered to bring someone in to help her. But she had come to Palermo originally prepared to handle these things on her own. It was pointless to change course now. She knew how to make herself look presentable. The colorful American artist—quite the oddity in these circles of sleek, sophisticated Europeans. And yet, she kind of liked it. Feeling different. Feeling special. She didn't mind the attention or the looks—maybe because she believed in her art. Believed in herself.

She *knew* what she created was good, interesting. The mix of paint and embroidery methods and the juxtaposition of whimsy and darkness, like all the fairy tales she'd grown up loving.

And even if no one else agreed with her, she created what she liked. What moved her. If it wasn't enough to support Gio, she'd simply go get a job.

Except you have his billionaire father involved now.

So there was that.

It was funny. She didn't feel like an oddity here in Lorenzo's gigantic, opulent house. She didn't have the same discomfort her parents did at the overt displays of wealth. It just felt…right. Like it reflected the man and his personality—and both those things were meant for her.

Ugh. They were very clearly not *meant* for each other, even if she could convince Lorenzo of the possibility of *meant for.* So...how did this go? After her art show, when she didn't have to be in Palermo anymore? Once Lorenzo dealt with the paparazzi and his rival and it was safe for her and Gio to return to America?

What happened once this was over? How did she move forward with Lorenzo as Gio's *involved* father? How did she move forward with her parents, who had stepped in and been everything she'd needed since they'd learned of Gio's existence?

What happened when Lorenzo brought *dates* to art shows or family Christmases and she was just supposed to accept it and think it was *great*?

She tried not to scowl as she fixed the rollers in her hair. The man wanted to bring a *date.* When clearly *something* still flashed between the two of them—even if it couldn't go anywhere.

No. That wasn't accurate. He wouldn't *let* it go anywhere. Because he viewed love as a fairy tale, and that fairy tales were bad.

Could that really be the whole story? Why did he care what she felt if he didn't believe in love? Why couldn't she love him and he just take it? Not that she'd told him or asked him for anything... No, she couldn't do that.

She looked at herself in the mirror. Dress on,

makeup done. The only thing she was waiting on was her hair.

She knew he found her attractive. He certainly hadn't planned office floor seductions even if he wasn't opposed to them. He'd likely come to that initial art show to see if the spark still flamed between them.

But he had walked away once. *Something* had sent him away from all that very good and very available sex. Abruptly. In the middle of the night.

She sighed heavily. At some point, she had to stop having these circular thoughts. She had to stop being desperate and hoping for something to change. Lorenzo might find her attractive, might not be opposed to sex, but he didn't want a relationship. And she had to put Gio before her own wants, her own weaknesses.

Or you could be honest with Lorenzo.

The idea filled her with such dread and fear, and the certainty it would ruin *everything*, that she immediately shoved it away.

The next step after tonight was clear. She and Lorenzo would sit down and hammer out a parental agreement. Maybe she would find a way to stay in Palermo so such agreements didn't involve international travel. Maybe her parents would even be amenable to moving here. They'd always wanted to travel Europe and had never had the chance.

She and Lorenzo would work it out, figure it out. As *parents. Not* former lovers...no matter how recently they'd been grappling about on his office floor.

She unrolled the curlers and finished her hair, determined that she was a strong, capable woman who would do what was best for her son. Ill-advised *almost* sex in offices notwithstanding.

A knock sounded at her door before she could go through another cycle of self-recrimination. Before she could offer a "come in" the door opened and Lorenzo stepped inside.

She frowned at him, though she did not scold him for violating her privacy. It *was* his house after all.

He looked her up and down, something flaring in his eyes that had heat pooling in her belly. When his dark eyes met hers again, there was an intensity there that she felt burn through her.

Not here. Not now. You cannot keep doing this, Brianna. She told herself this, over and over again, but she knew…all it would take was a touch. That was how weak she was. If there was a way to fight that, she hadn't found it.

"I'll go with you."

He said it so…fiercely her heart tripped over itself. And worse, she felt that sensual haze threaten to invade her brain. But she was reminded of his plan to bring a *date*, and that was just enough figurative cold water to remind herself how to behave.

"Lorenzo, you made it very clear you do not wish us to be seen together. I do not see why you would come with me when you've made other plans."

"You cannot wear that and…"

She raised an eyebrow when he didn't finish, standing in her doorway looking like a storm. "And what?" she asked, looking down at the deep red, one-shouldered dress that hugged her curves in a very flattering manner. She felt like a goddess in this dress.

His expression was hard, but his eyes glittered with that same *lust* they had almost acted on yesterday in his office.

You cannot give in to that, Brianna. Not tonight. Not without him admitting some feelings. Not without him giving an inch or two.

She considered that. Did he *have* feelings for her? *Could* he? It was the *could* that had her turning to face him fully. That had her asking the one thing she hadn't asked yet. "Can you answer me one thing? Truthfully?"

"I suppose that depends."

"Why did you leave me the way that you did two years ago? Snuck away in the middle of the night like a coward when I know you aren't one." His expression hardened even more at the word *coward*. "No word. No explanation."

His mouth got very stern. "Because the relationship had run its course."

"And that didn't warrant a discussion? Because that might have been *your* conclusion, but it wasn't mine. *I* was blindsided."

"I have no use for postmortems, Brianna. I am a busy man. I had business to attend to in Palermo and did not have time to deal with hysterical women in Florence."

She should not find that funny. It should be so

arrogant and offensive, the way he said it with such complete authority. Like of course she'd be hysterical. "Do most women you break things off with rend garments, wailing at your feet and carrying on?"

His mouth curved, ever so slightly at the corner. All dark amusement. "You would be surprised, *dusci.*"

She tried not to scowl or smile and just remain neutral, but, oh, the man was arrogant. And probably right. Worse, she didn't know how she might have behaved if he'd broken things off to her face. She had been young and naive and desperately in love with him. She'd love to believe her pride would have seen her through, but…well, best not to dwell on it. What *would* have been did not matter in the here and now.

"You know, there was quite a lot of time to think when I was pregnant. To go over it in my head. I came up with all sorts of reasons for why you left."

"Do you not have an event to get to?" he returned coolly. But that arrogant quirk of the mouth was gone. Like she'd gotten to him. Like this conversation might make him *uncomfortable.*

The thought emboldened her. "You know, some men leave their partners because they are scared by the depth and breadth of their feelings."

If possible, his expression got even more remote. He voiced no admissions, no denials. Just cool disdain.

Brianna had to wonder if that was an answer in it of itself. Her heart twisted in a hope she knew was foolish but couldn't quash. So she continued on, wanting to find some chink in his armor of stoicism. "They can't handle how much they've come to care for and rely on the person, so they leave. Disappear." And of course *some* men were just assholes, but she wasn't trying to make that point in the moment.

Because she didn't think he was one, even when he wanted to be. Not to other people. The man might hide it, but he cared too much about *people*.

Still, she expected his response to be a laugh. A cruel joke. Something scathing enough that she'd stop talking about it. She expected him to put her very firmly in her place.

But he only turned and left, and Brianna...didn't have the first clue what to do with that.

Lorenzo didn't often attend events alone. He had a small group of women who were happy to accompany him anywhere at a moment's notice just to be seen on his arm or get into an exclusive event they might not have received an invite to. This group of women didn't get ideas, and he did not see "dates" with them as anything more than a business arrangement.

Neither did they.

These women never spoke of feelings. They never pressed for more. They were in it to boost their profiles and nothing more. He preferred these kinds of dates for business events, and this tonight was business. Maybe not in the traditional sense, but in the sense that he had to think of it like business.

Cold. Calculated. And nothing to do with the roiling, jagged things fighting for purchase inside of him after that little conversation with Brianna.

Which was why he'd obtained a date even though he'd decided against it earlier. When he'd walked into Brianna's room and seen her in that *dress*. That deep red. The way her body shimmered. Like sex itself.

The thought of her attending the event alone, a sheep to the wolves essentially, had torn him up inside. It wasn't jealousy, he told himself. Just…common sense. There would be men there and she was the mother of his child.

So he'd made the impulsive offer to go with her. Or maybe it was a demand. He didn't really remember past the punch of seeing her. The desire to touch her and forget *everything else*.

But then she'd started talking about ancient history. About feelings and leaving and… Well, it had reminded him where he got when he did things impulsively. Somewhere ridiculous.

So he'd gone back to the original plan. The calculated plan. A date. So he could protect her, and keep his distance.

Honestly, he deserved her gratitude, not her foolish questioning.

That hit far too close to home.

He scowled at himself as he strode up to his date's building. The doorman nodded him inside and when he knocked on her door, she opened it with her famous sultry smile.

"Natalia," he greeted, forcing his mouth to curve though it did not want to. "You look beautiful this evening."

She offered her hand and he brushed a perfunctory kiss against the knuckles. She wore a slinky black dress and smoky dark makeup. He should have been immediately distracted from the pop of color that Brianna had been.

But all he could think about was the way the red had made her skin glow. The way her blue eyes were dark and warm and full of so many things.

"I was surprised to hear from you," Natalia said, grabbing a handbag and a wrap. "This isn't our typical kind of event. I didn't know you had any interest in the arts."

They walked to his car, and he tried to focus on the dark, alluring promise that was Natalia. Not sunlight. Not warmth. Not the weight of Gio in his arms while a tear slid down Brianna's cheek.

This was growing harder and harder and he could not imagine why. He could not *accept* why. He was in charge of his mind. His thoughts, his choices. Feelings were of little consequence to a man of his superior control.

"I have an interest in many things," he said, trying to sound his charming self. But the words sounded brittle even to his own ears.

They rode to the art gallery where Brianna's artwork was the main event. She had made quite a splash at the first event, and her manager was eager to get her back into the studio. Lorenzo would need to create her an art studio on the property. She would need to get back to creating as she was going to be in high demand in short time.

What's the plan there? Keep her and her parents at your estate forever?

No, they would need their own place. But on the grounds. Close. So Gio was always within reach.

Well, why couldn't they all live in the same house? It would be easy. Best for Gio. Best for all of them. Maybe it wasn't the common thing to do in such a situation, but he wasn't trying to be common any more than he was trying to be traditional.

However, if he kept Brianna in his house, he would need to ensure that did not create too much interest or speculation. *Or temptation.* He'd need a wife. To convince everyone that it wasn't what it looked like. That they were very modern and accepting. A *blended* family.

He glanced at Natalia. She knew how to act, work angles. Maybe she wasn't exactly the perfect wife material, but she had a keen mind. If he could convince her this was in her best interest—if he could *make* a union in her best interest—he could have this settled soon.

You know, some men leave their partners because they are scared by the depth and breadth of their feelings.

Brianna's voice echoed in his mind. The image of her in that dress burnt into his mind no matter how he tried to erase it.

The sooner he had a wife in place, the better.

He helped Natalia out of the car and took her arm as he led her into the art gallery. He saw Brianna immediately in that brilliant red. And, as if she was keenly attuned to him, she looked over her shoulder and unerringly found him.

Their gazes met across the room. He watched the shock hit her. Convinced himself the dark thrill that wound through him was simply satisfaction of a plan well made. He would keep his eye on her, and no one would speculate. *That* was why his body reacted.

Not her beauty. Not the little flash of jealousy he saw there in her eyes before the person she'd been talking to regained her attention and she looked away.

Then snuck glances at his date as they made their way around the room.

Something like satisfaction swept through him. That she watched. That she cared. That she didn't like it.

Except, no. She had to like it. She had to agree. She had to understand if his plan was to work. He'd make her understand. Somehow. He would have a wife and Brianna could… She could certainly…

But even the thought of another man looking at her twisted a deep, dangerous jealousy inside of him. He knew where these feelings led. He had to eradicate them.

"Lorenzo."

He was still looking at Brianna, but he got the sense Natalia had been trying to get his attention for some time. He managed to tear his gaze away from all that red and smiled at Natalia.

"She's lovely," Natalia said, gesturing toward Brianna. "I've seen the stories. Do you really have a child together?"

He found himself hesitant to bring Gio into this. "Does it matter?"

"Of course not. I'm only curious."

"Dante's trying to wage yet another war against me using my son and his mother. He won't win." And there was a war inside of himself that he had to fight. He forced his mouth to curve at his date. "How do you feel about marriage, Natalia?"

She laughed, low and throaty. "Oh, Lorenzo. You're such an idiot sometimes."

He frowned in utter shock. Natalia always spoke her mind but calling him an *idiot* was over-the-top. "I would make it worth your while."

"Of course you would. But what would make you think I'd whore myself out in such a fashion?"

That word left him utterly cold. "Never that."

She made a considering noise. "Regardless. I'm not interested in marrying you, darling. Maybe if I thought it *was* business and not just a powerful man's cowardice, we'd have something to talk about. But I won't be any coward's shield."

There was that word again. First Brianna, now Natalia. When he'd never had the *opportunity* to be a coward. For as long as he could remember, he'd had to be the brave one. *He'd* had to have the courage to do the hard things. Pay bills. Plan funerals.

Build empires so nothing would ever touch his family again. "You have a lot of negative opinions of me this evening, *darling*," he managed to say without *too* much acid in his tone.

She shook her head. "No. I can just see through you this evening and you don't like it. I'm usually not the one men use for a distraction, and I'm trying not to be bitter about it because we've always gotten along well. But heed my advice, Lorenzo. You need to deal with her. Not me."

"I have dealt with her, thank you," he replied stiffly.

"Lorenzo," Natalia said quietly. Almost like a friend breaking bad news. "You're not even looking at me."

He managed to rip his gaze away from Brianna. Again. Focus on Natalia. "I need a business partner."

She shook her head. "You need a reality check." She reached up and patted his cheek. "And I am not part of that reality."

CHAPTER ELEVEN

BRIANNA DID NOT care that he was here. She did not care about the gorgeous beauty on his arm. She didn't *care*. She was above Lorenzo and his dates and plans. She was here for *Brianna*.

She had people interested in her process. In her *motifs*. Her damn inspiration. She did not need Lorenzo's interest. His concern. His...whatever this was.

She hoped he had a wonderful time with his date. She hoped he fell in love with the woman.

Love is a lie.

If only *she* could believe that as vehemently as he did. If only anything she felt for him settled in her like a *lie*. Instead it was like some core tenet of everything she was. Loving him was in her blood and she couldn't get it out.

Worse, the way he'd walked out of her bedroom earlier, without refuting a single thing she'd said. Letting her think he loved her too was the worst kind of torture.

She tried to focus on the conversations around her,

but her eyes wandered. Always veering straight for him. *Them*, because his date was always with him. And every single time she looked over, he wasn't gazing at said date. He wasn't cuddled together with the woman on his arm.

No, every time Brianna looked over, he was looking right back at her. And every *single* time a jolt went through her whole body. Every time she found herself fantasizing about him striding through the room and coming over to her and…

But he wasn't *with* her. He was with this…woman. Beautiful. *Tall*. Perfect. He didn't believe in love. Whatever he felt for her didn't matter to him because he was here with a date. They were a striking couple, really.

She hoped they both choked on their champagne.

She closed her eyes for a moment, trying to get a hold of her whirling feelings. She needed to find somewhere where she *couldn't* look at them. Because honestly, her feelings weren't the fault or responsibility of that woman, or even Lorenzo. Her feelings, her desire, her desperate wish he could believe in love were hers and hers alone.

Brianna made her way through the party, eyeing the balcony that looked out over the sparkling Palermo. Some fresh air, some distance, and she would find a way to get herself under control. She was strong. She'd had to be over the past two years. It couldn't dissolve just because Lorenzo was back in her life.

Maybe this would all be easier if he hated her. If

he told her in no uncertain terms he would never love her. *Maybe*. But maybe it would just…all be hard, and she had to find some way to deal with it better than she had been.

There were people out here on the balcony, but not as many as inside. She wished she could escape the low buzz of conversation, but Brianna found a little shadowed area of the balcony where it at least felt like she was alone. The cool air against her hot cheeks. The stars above.

She had to find some inner strength out here. But it was hard. Because she did not understand him. There was a piece to his thought process she was clearly missing, and he wasn't about to share it with her.

No, he preferred to come into her bedroom, claiming he'd go with her. Refusing to answer questions about why he'd broken things off with her. Then showing up here with a date.

Was he trying to make her jealous? Was he stooping to something so childish? Or did he really think so little about her and what she might feel, that he couldn't fathom why this would hurt?

Worse, was it some combination of all those? Complicated and messy. Not so easily defined. Like everything swirling inside of her.

"Ms. Andersen, I am surprised to find you hiding in the dark. This is not quite the cheerful image of the artist we've been fed," a man's voice said.

Brianna looked over at the form that approached. She knew her manager had introduced her to this

man at the cocktail party the other night, but that
entire event was a blur and she didn't remember his
name. Still, she smiled politely. "Art isn't always
cheerful. Even mine."

"But I am fascinated by the cheer in it neverthe-
less."

"That's very kind." She tried to focus on the man,
her art, this conversation. Forget everything else.
"It's important to me that no matter how macabre the
subject matter, the end result doesn't become bleak."
Her core life belief. One it would do some good to
remind herself of in the midst of this little pity party.

"I think that's what makes it so powerful. I particularly enjoyed the piece you had titled *Sunset Mel-
ancholy*. But someone has bought it out from under
me."

It was the exact distraction she needed. Talk of
her art. Talk of people *buying* her pieces. Lorenzo
wasn't out here and this man had clearly inspected
her work enough to really be able to talk about it,
so she could get lost in discussion of craft. He was
flirting with her, underneath all these compliments
he showered on her as the conversation continued.
She wasn't so naive she didn't understand that, but
that too was a distraction.

Full minutes passed as she talked with the man.
She didn't flirt back, but she didn't end the conversation either. It was a breath of fresh air that she didn't
feel the need to search out Lorenzo. She could just
stand here and talk.

So it figured that Lorenzo would then approach,

bringing that small moment of respite to a crashing halt.

"Calo. How good to see you," Lorenzo said, without even excusing himself for interrupting the conversation. He thrust a hand toward the man as he came to stand next to Brianna.

The man in question turned his attention from Brianna and gave Lorenzo a vague kind of smile and shook the offered hand. "Ah, Mr. Parisi. It's been a while."

"Yes, it has." Lorenzo was every inch the smiling businessman, but Brianna definitely picked up on something less than friendly between the two. "Will you excuse us, Calo? I have something private I wish to discuss with Brianna."

"Of course," the man replied. He offered Brianna a smile and began to say something, but Lorenzo took her by the arm and led her away. Back into the main room of the party, then into a hallway. Away from people.

Brianna didn't jerk her arm out of his grasp. She wouldn't cause a scene, though she considered doing so. But what would that serve? They were trying to *avoid* too much paparazzi attention.

So why is he anywhere near you?

"Where's your date, Lorenzo?" she asked, trying to keep the jealousy out of her tone as he drew her into a darkened room. Even if she felt jealous, she knew there was nothing productive about this feeling.

But if he had sex with that woman, she'd want to

tear her hair out. That was just how she felt, whether she wanted to or not.

That all being true, she still understood the *whys* of him bringing a date. And those *whys* didn't make sense if he was going to drag her into darkened rooms.

"Never mind that," he said, turning to face her in the very dim light. He crossed his arms over his chest and looked down at her, expression thunderous. "You can thank me for saving you from that man."

For a moment, she could only stare up at him. Shock held her utterly mute. Could he truly be so out of touch with reality? "Saving me?" she finally managed, though her voice was strangled. "I was having a nice conversation with a man interested in buying one of my pieces."

"I am sure he was interested in *something*," Lorenzo returned acidly.

Acid. Anger. Because she'd…had an innocent conversation with a man? Fury erupted within her. "Let me get this straight. You get to bring a date to *my* art show, but I can't even have a conversation with a man? Lorenzo, you can't be serious."

"I know that man," he said, pointing back toward the event she could no longer see or hear. "I know what he's after."

"Oh. Do you? Perhaps you should be more worried about yourself, *dusci*," she said, trotting out that little term as if turnabout would somehow make this all fair play. But none of it was fair, and she was so… mad about that. At him. At the situation. At herself.

"About what *you're* after. Because your actions are not matching your words."

"Three years ago I fired him, Brianna. Now he works for Dante Marino. The man bound and determined to make our son a target. I have kept that from happening, and will continue to do so, but you cannot be so…so…naive."

Naive.

"Oh, so flirting with me is his great revenge? Explain that to me, Lorenzo, when you don't even care about me. You brought a date. The whole idea is to make certain no one thinks there's anything remotely romantic going on between us. A man flirting with me—regardless of what he's after—suits your little narrative, does it not?"

His mouth firmed at that.

"You're, in fact, ruining your own plan by talking to me. By taking me off to this isolated room where no one can see us. If people noticed, don't you think they'll talk? Don't you think they'll wonder why you left your date to pull me away from a very *nice* man complimenting me about my art?"

"I don't care what people think."

She laughed, and she knew it was a tad high-pitched, maybe even borderline hysterical. But the man was driving her insane. On multiple levels. And still, in spite of all of that, she wanted to be right here. Talking to him—not…whatever the other man's name was. Not her manager. Not anyone but Lorenzo.

She wanted to know what Lorenzo thought of her

latest piece. She wanted to hear him speak of his family, or she wanted to tell him a funny Gio story. She wanted to kiss him. To find a way back to Florence and those two blissful months she still looked back on as some of the best days of her life.

She still felt like that woman in a sense, but she wasn't. Because that had been before Gio. She was the same person in so many ways, but she'd grown. Matured.

Had Lorenzo? He hadn't known he had a son. He hadn't had a broken heart. He'd walked away scot-free and now some of the consequences were at his door. Was he exactly the same man he'd been? Would he change?

Could he change?

She studied him in the dim light. So full of restrained frustration. She *almost* felt sorry for him. He had taken Gio in with open arms. He was made to be a father after all, but that didn't mean he'd dealt with any of the emotional implications. No, he was too busy plotting and planning what the future would look like. Too busy thwarting Dante Marino's attempts to ruin his reputation.

He was trying to wrestle the world under his control, and he was very good at it. But there were things you could never fully control. Namely other people.

He thought he could though, didn't he? Control her. The woman he'd brought. The narrative of how people thought of him in regards to his *enterprises* and what he wished to do there.

The only reason Brianna was back in his orbit

was because of their child, so he would mold her into the life *he* wanted…with no concern to her own wants. No concern to anything except his precious *plans* and *control.*

He dictated who she spoke to. *He* dictated what events they were allowed to be seen at together. *He* alone made the choices.

She could love him and still know that was no way to live.

"I am not some toy, some possession, Lorenzo. I never have been. Maybe that's why you left me the way you did. Because you could not control how I would react. You could not put a neat little bow on it if I had a chance to have a say in it." She preferred the dream world where he left because he simply loved her too much, but this one made a lot more sense.

He scoffed. "You are obsessed with the past."

Which was interesting because it was still not agreement or denial. Every time she brought up two years ago, he evaded. Would she ever understand what had happened or would he always leave her wondering?

It didn't matter. *She* knew she had no control over the world and most especially other people. That was a major lesson in motherhood.

"No, Lorenzo. Not obsessed. I'm working *through* the past. Working through the events that shaped me, that still affect me emotionally. It's healthy, actually. Necessary to adapt and grow. I'd suggest you do the same, but I know how you'll respond to that."

"The past is gone. We must prepare for the future."

"Ah, the future. Let me guess." She crossed her arms over her chest to mimic his pose. To meet his cold decisiveness with a frigid dismissiveness. "You know exactly how that's going to go."

"Yes, as a matter of fact. I have a plan."

He looked so…royal. Standing there tall and shoulders back. Expression remote, but with a confidence that never seemed to shake. She should not find it appealing. Should not be distracted by the shape of his mouth, the intensity in his eyes.

So she tried to focus on how she felt about his *plans*. "I'm eager to hear it. You'll have a hard time walking out in the middle of the night when I'm staying at your estate, Lorenzo. What are you going to do? Escape to Florence this time when things get a little too real?"

He said nothing to that. Nor did he leave. Maybe he was not as in control as he liked to believe. Or she did.

"Go on then. Lay this plan on me. If not escape, what's next? How is our future going to go, oh, Wise One?"

"Now is not the time or the place."

She leaned forward, ignored the punch of the scent of his expensive cologne. The low twist in her belly that somehow seemed more potent and dangerous with all this anger whirling around inside of her. "Oh, it's exactly the time and place. Tell me, Lorenzo. What's the plan? What's my future?"

"Honestly, Brianna."

He made a move as if to leave. After dragging

her here. After interrupting her conversation. All dismissive arrogance. Oh, no. She all but jumped in front of him, barring him from exit unless he bodily moved her.

He could, she knew, but he was being so very careful she got the feeling he did not want to touch her.

And what did *that* mean?

"Tell me, Lorenzo. What's my future?"

"Very well. It is simple. You will stay in Palermo, on my estate, as will your parents, should they be amenable. You will have your own space, an art studio, and whatever else you require. This way, Gio will never feel as if he's being shuttled back and forth between two different families." He recited these all as though they were facts. Set in stone. Already a foregone conclusion.

All that certainty that should make her volcanic, but Brianna had nothing smart to say to that. She *wanted* to be angry, but it was… It was everything she wanted. For Gio.

For yourself.

She blinked at that. Why did she want to stay and keep putting herself through this? The same estate? So close to this man when he couldn't admit anything about what he felt?

She couldn't believe love was a lie, because to her way of thinking, love was the only thing powerful enough to make an otherwise intelligent woman this stupid and willing to torture herself.

"It will go quite well. A modern solution. Then,

to ensure it is seen as such, I will be married by the
end of next year to an appropriate wife and step-
mother to Gio."

Married. *Step*mother.

Because this *appropriate* wife would not be her.

The pain of the blow was truly astonishing. She
should have been ready for it. But in one breath he
was building her dream life—staying close for Gio's
sake, an art studio for her. But in this dream life he
was creating, he would be married to someone *else*.

She wanted to *weep*. Which she would decidedly
not do in front of him. Not when he expected her
to just…live on the same estate? Accept this as in-
disputable fact when the woman he was going to
marry didn't even *exist*. Unless it was the woman
out there…

Whom he'd paid very little attention to. He'd been
looking at *Brianna* all night. Instead of engaging in
conversation with his date, he was too busy dragging Brianna away from nice men making pleasant
conversation.

So she didn't crumble at the idea of him marrying
someone else and her just having to take it. Not yet.
Because he wasn't claiming to *love* someone else.
He was just building empires. Maybe it hurt. Maybe
she thought him a complete and utter fool. But she
could fight it if it wasn't about *love*.

She lifted her chin, still blocking his exit. "What
about me?"

"What about *you*?" he returned coolly.

"Am I allowed to marry in this scenario?"

There was a long, stretched-out silence as a muscle ticked in his jaw. When he spoke, it sounded strangled. "As long as I approve of the groom."

This was enough to make her laugh, rather than cry. But before she could say anything, he continued.

"This is how it will be. You can argue with me. You can whine about it, but in the end, you will see, it is best and that's what will happen."

"You are an idiot, Lorenzo. Delusional or too arrogant to function, or both."

"I grow tired of this insult hurled at me this evening."

Brianna laughed. Again. Honestly, even with her heart cracking into a million pieces, the whole farce was hilarious. "Did it ever occur to you that everyone insulting you is *correct* if there's consensus?"

The expression on his face was such that it appeared he had *not* considered that. "I've had quite enough, Brianna. So move."

"But you brought me here. To shout at me about my naive choices in having conversations with men at an art show in which my *job* is to talk about my art. Tell me, Lorenzo, what did you expect to happen when you dragged me into this dim room, alone?"

"I expected to have a rational conversation. Clearly you're in no headspace for that, so I will leave you alone."

Her hand curled into a fist. She wanted to punch him. She really did. But that wouldn't get through to him. Nothing would. So why not be as *irrational* as she wanted? "Make me move then, Lorenzo."

He took her by the arm. But he did not move her. He didn't even pull. His hand just gripped her, branded her like an iron. Oh, how she wanted this infuriating, ridiculous idiot of a man. It would never make sense to her how easily he affected her.

Never, she thought, as his grip finally moved her. Not out of the way. Not away from him.

No, he jerked her to him in a move that had her crashing against the hard mountain of him. Before his mouth crashed to hers.

It was wild. Explosive. Rough and wonderful… and if she had even a shred of intelligence or self-preservation, she would push him away. She would end this ridiculous cycle of stupidity.

But she didn't. She held on. Clutched him like her life depended on it. Returned the furious kiss with one of her own. Because all that feeling climbed inside of her. It rushed through her like a drug. *Here* he admitted he loved her, even if he didn't believe in love. Even if he never said the words.

When he kissed her, when he touched her, when they came together as nothing but bodies seeking pleasure, she *felt* his love for her.

She *knew* she had to tell him to stop, because he'd never admit it or acknowledge that love. She knew kissing him back, wrapping herself around him was the kind of mindless lack of thought that had gotten her into this whole mess in the first place.

But his hands slid up the slit in her skirt, pushing the fabric up. It was dark in here, so she couldn't see him, but she knew him. His mouth, his hands, the shape of his body. She knew how to arch against him, how to nip at his jaw, how to curl her fingers into his hair.

His mouth streaked down her neck, bringing the strap down over her shoulder, cool air touching bared skin. She had to stop this before it went too far. Because...because...

"You have a date here. You brought someone else. She..." Brianna tried to find the words. To tell him it was wrong. To tell herself. She had stopped this once before. She had to be strong enough to stop it again.

"She knows what this is, Brianna." His eyes were dark blazes of fire. His words growled. He was intensity personified. Everything she wanted. "She has no designs on me."

"Lucky her." Because Brianna didn't have the first clue what this was. What to do about it.

Except succumb.

CHAPTER TWELVE

THE THOUGHT OF another man putting his hands on Brianna had consumed Lorenzo from the moment he'd seen her in that dress. Being at this party, seeing other men look at her, it destroyed him. Whether it be that ineffectual weasel Calo Finetti or another man, Brianna was *his*, and anyone else so much as having a *thought* about her sent a fury through him he knew would destroy everything.

It wasn't that he didn't understand it was hypocritical to consider marrying another woman while hating the idea Brianna might marry someone else. Touch them. Be naked with them. He knew it was absolutely wrong and unfair.

He just didn't care. Not in this moment, when she was arguing with him looking like sunlight in a dim room. So that no matter what realities and truths existed, he only knew he needed her. He knew this dark ribbon of emotion inside of him was only cured if his mouth was on hers.

It made everything else disappear. Nothing mattered here with her mouth on his. Not tabloids. Certainly not Natalia and her refusals. Not Dante Marino or anyone else.

Brianna's mouth. Her arms around him. The sunshine sweetness of her even when she was angry with him.

She didn't push him away. Didn't refuse him. She kissed him back with the same wild desperation that had taken hold of every rational thought, every careful plan.

The plan was gone. Everything was gone except the velvet of her skin, the way she begged him.

Because she was begging him. For more. For all. He closed the door to the room, plunging them into darkness. He shoved the skirt of her dress up, found the soft, wet heat of her. Touched her there until her breath shuddered.

The scent of her filled the room. His body so hard he did not know if he would ever move again. Everything centered on Brianna. His sweet, beautiful Brianna, moving against his hand.

"Lorenzo. Please."

Please.

He freed himself. There was no time for finesse. He ached. Until there was nothing left but the ache. But her.

They both needed something more than gentleness. They needed the wild. To feed the desperation. So he drove himself home, as she wrapped herself around him. He used the wall for leverage, tried to calm the frantic panic inside of him with a demanding pace.

He was inside her. In this dark room. He couldn't see her, but he could feel her. Every breath. Every squeeze of her fingers against his shoulders. The arch of her back as she opened for him, took him deeper.

She shuddered out her first release, clutching him. He wished he could see her. He wished he could take his time. He wished...

For all those dangerous things. What they'd had before. The sweetness of it. The joy of it. When every time they'd come together felt like coming home.

And you know where all that leads.

In this moment he didn't care. He pulled down the strap of her dress until he freed her taut nipple. He bent his head and tasted. Licked, nipped. Until she was gasping, begging, writhing against him.

Wild. Wanton. His. His blood roared. His body throbbed for her and her alone. To the point of pain, and that pain was joy as long as he was inside of her. As long as her arms were around him and she panted his name.

Mine. Mine. Mine.

He wasn't sure if those chanted words were thoughts or something he verbalized but he didn't care because she could not be anyone else's. Ever.

So he made her his. Over and over again. With his hands, his mouth, his body. Until she was sobbing out his name. *His* name and only his.

Until he lost himself. Over that edge and into nothing but pleasure and release. His breath was ragged, and he held her there against the wall for long, pulsing seconds as they both tried to recover.

He didn't let his brain shift into gear. Then the thoughts would start. The recriminations. The reason. He couldn't go down that road just yet. Not with his blood still roaring in his ears. Not with a warm and sated Brianna limp in his arms.

He stayed in this moment, in this warmth. *In this love*.

The word love was always the antidote, and he began to extricate himself. There *was* a world outside this room. He smoothed down her dress, still in the dark, doing everything by feel alone. He tucked himself away, but he did not let her go. Did not step away.

Once he did…reality would come crashing down and—

"Lorenzo," she said in a pained whisper. She sounded on the verge of tears and nothing could have pierced him more. "I cannot keep doing this with you."

It was strange. He'd meant to say those exact words once he had his faculties back. To gently put her in her place. To accept *some* responsibility, but certainly not all.

But her saying the exact words he'd been thinking, when she sounded so hurt, twisted something inside of him.

The words made him angry even though he agreed.

She should want to keep doing it. They were amazing at *it*, and that was all she should be thinking about.

"I need to go home," she continued, sounding no less devastated.

"I'll have my driver take you back at once," he said, angry at himself that his voice sounded so weak. That he *felt* weak. That he wanted to offer her a million reassuring words and, worse, feelings.

Love is a lie. Love is destruction. Lorenzo, what have you done?

"No, Lorenzo. I need to go *home*. Gio and I need to go back to New Jersey."

The words simply did not compute. He tried to look at her, read her expression, but it was still nothing but darkness in the room.

"I'm not saying the two of you shouldn't have a relationship," she continued. "I don't want to keep you from him. We'll have to work out some kind of custody agreement. You're a billionaire. You should be able to fly to the States as much as you want."

No words could have shocked him more, and he was still struggling to get his mind to return to reality. "Brianna." He was trying to sound stern. He had a bad feeling he was failing. When he never failed.

Couldn't allow himself to fail ever again.

"I can't do this. I can't watch you marry another woman. I can't keep…trying to resist you. Clearly, I can't do it for long. I do not know how to fight how much I want you, and before you say that's just fine, it isn't. If you don't want a relationship, it isn't *fine* for me. The only way I survive this is distance."

Survive this.

The brokenness in her voice, or maybe the dark,

or maybe the way his heart felt bruised at the idea of her leaving had him reliving old moments he'd like to forget.

I can't survive this, Lorenzo. I can't bear it.

Rocca. His sweet sister who'd become so broken. So lost. The perfect image of his mother. They'd both paid the price for all that *love*.

He stepped away from Brianna, a cold ice trickling through him. It made his fingers feel thick and incapable of doing something as simple as opening the door.

I can't bear it. I can't bear it.

And then she hadn't. Because love broke things. It broke people. Crushed them into bits until they couldn't bear it. Until they made all the wrong choices. Wrung themselves out. It hurt until there was nothing left. Until they were gone.

He could tell himself it wasn't true, but his love for Brianna existed within him no matter how hard he denied it. No matter how many plans he could make to wed someone else. These horrible feelings would always be inside him. So she was right. Distance was the best option.

I can't bear it.

Distance was the only option to save Brianna.

"All right," he managed to say. "Give me a few days to ensure you and Gio will be safe and then we'll make the arrangements for you to return to America."

"Thank you." Her inhale was so shaky he stepped away. He gave her the distance she needed. In the interim between now and when she could safely return to New Jersey, he would give her all the distance she asked.

He would not break her. He would not let his love break her, or hers break her. Perhaps she had the right of it with this…distance. He could accept this. He would.

He would make it right. Keep everyone safe. He would not fail again. He couldn't. For his son. For himself.

For Brianna.

What Brianna really wanted was to go back to Lorenzo's estate. Pack everyone up and head to the airport. Safety and all else be damned. She had to get away from him.

Or her feelings for him. Her weakness when it came to him. She didn't know what she was really running away from except maybe her own failures.

She did not understand her utter lack of control when it came to this man. It was one thing to love him when he didn't—or wouldn't—love her back. It was another thing to just…have sex with him. In the middle of a *party*? Knowing he wanted to marry someone else. Who did that? What kind of woman, what kind of mother did it make her?

Maybe it should have been some comfort that he seemed to have the same problem resisting when it came to her, but all she could think about was the way he'd left her before.

If she stayed, if she kept putting herself in a posi-

tion to fall deeper and deeper in love with him, forever bending when it came to him—even when he
came to *her* event with a *date*—she would break,
and she couldn't.

She had a son who depended on her. Who loved
her. She had to put him first. And herself.

She didn't have to worry about money anymore.
Lorenzo would take care of Gio financially, probably to the point of spoiling. But she still needed a
career. To support herself. To feel fulfilled.

So she forced herself to return to the party. She
did not pay attention to what Lorenzo did. She was
afraid she would start bawling in the middle of the
art show, and that was enough to keep her will power
intact.

Lucky her.

She spoke to a few more people who'd bought
pieces. She smiled, hopefully. When she finally
thought she'd stayed long enough, she went and
found her manager to say her goodbyes.

"This has been such a success, Brianna," her manager said warmly, pumping her hands in a shake. "I
hear you might be staying in Palermo longer. We
could have another show next week. I could see about
getting you some studio space and—"

"No. No, Juliette. As much as that sounds wonderful, I really need to get home. Spend some time
there. In my home studio."

Juliette nodded, though her smile had dimmed.
"Very well. We'll get the final numbers to you to-

morrow, and the payments will be over the next few weeks."

Brianna thanked her, then collected her things and left. It was still a *little* early, but not unforgivably so. She happened to see Lorenzo out of the corner of her eye as she exited the main room, but she refused to turn her head and look to see what his expression was, who was on his arm.

Hopefully, he stayed. Hopefully, he and his date made whatever gossip story suited Lorenzo's plan and vision.

I will be married by the end of next year to an appropriate wife.

She would not torture herself by wondering why *she* couldn't be the perfect wife. It wouldn't matter to her in a few days. She'd be home in New Jersey, getting over him just as she had two years ago.

But you didn't get over him.

What a depressing thought. Brianna watched the city pass outside the car window. Over the past two years she'd pushed her heartbreak away by loving Gio. By putting those jagged feelings into her art.

So she'd do it again. Focus on being a mother. Put her pain into her art. Maybe it wouldn't solve the problem of being irrevocably in love with Lorenzo, but at least it was productive.

Except this time around, she would have to see him. She would have to co-parent with him. She couldn't even resist him when he brought another woman to *her* art show—did she really think she was going to be able to control herself in a co-parenting situation?

She was exhausted when she arrived at the estate. Emotionally wrung out from berating herself for the entire rest of the evening. From smiling when she wanted to cry. From knowing she needed to go home to New Jersey, for telling Lorenzo she did, and then for wishing he'd argue with her. Beg her to stay.

You are pathetic, she chastised herself silently as she was let into the house.

She'd go upstairs, check on Gio and her parents. Then shower, sleep, and hope clarity arrived by morning.

But before she could go upstairs, she heard voices. This in itself wouldn't have stopped her, but she heard what could only be Gio's excited squeal.

Brianna frowned. Well, at least that gave her something to shift her upset toward. Gio should have been asleep a good hour ago. She marched toward the living room, ready to lecture her parents, though they likely didn't deserve it.

They sat on the couch in the main living room, and Gio stood behind a curtain clearly playing a game of peekaboo with... Not her parents, but a woman seated on the floor in the middle of the room.

The moment the woman turned her head to look at her, Brianna knew who she was. Not by name. Simply by looks. She *had* to be one of Lorenzo's sisters. Those dark eyes, that sharp nose. Something in the mouth. Oh, this woman was beautiful with her dark curly hair and expertly done makeup. There weren't just hints of Lorenzo on her face, but Gio as well.

The woman stood. She didn't smile Brianna's way. There was something speculative in her gaze even as Gio made a gurgling squeal and hurtled himself toward Brianna's frozen form.

One of Lorenzo's siblings. In the flesh. All the secrets this woman would know. Would she be able to explain him to Brianna? Tell Brianna what was wrong with her for being so desperately in love with a man who wanted nothing to do with it.

Why does he think love is a lie? What can I do to change his mind?

Brianna lifted Gio into her arms, knowing she couldn't ask this woman any of the questions she wanted to. Knowing she should greet her in some way but finding herself mute.

The woman also didn't offer any pleasantries. But she wasn't looking at Brianna anymore. She was looking behind her.

"Saverina. What are you doing here?" Lorenzo's dark voice said from right behind Brianna.

The girl sauntered over to where Brianna stood, then moved past her. Brianna turned and watched as the woman marched right up to Lorenzo in the doorway.

"Meeting my nephew, of course," the young woman said with an insouciant shrug. "And before you start nagging, you should know it was Stefano's idea and the rest of the family will be descending tomorrow."

Then she wrapped her arms around Lorenzo and squeezed. "Come now, *frati*. Welcome me home."

CHAPTER THIRTEEN

LIKE A PARENT, Lorenzo did not have favorites when it came to his siblings. But even he had to admit he had more of a soft spot for Saverina than the others. She had only been eight when their mother had died—and their mother had been less than helpful years before that. Saverina had just turned eleven when their father had also passed.

Lorenzo remembered holding her as an infant, more so than any of the others. Changing her diapers, feeding her meals. While most of his siblings were more like his children than his siblings, Saverina had never felt like anything other than his daughter.

His responsibility.

And here she was. Playing with Gio. Meeting Brianna. It was like two worlds clashing, and he wasn't ready for that. He hadn't planned or prepared. He hadn't found a way to erect all the necessary walls to make this…okay. That was why he had decidedly *not* invited his family to descend yet.

If he had wanted these worlds to mix already, he would have issued a family-wide invite. Hosted a dinner. He had planned to get to that point someday, but not until he was prepared.

But now Saverina was here with no warning, and he had to somehow juggle balls he wasn't ready to.

Worse, Brianna was standing there in her red dress, all sunshine and reminders of what happened when they were alone together. No control over themselves, over their emotions. At least at the party there'd been so much of their interaction in the dark. Now he was home and there were lights and her dark blue stare, full of pain, confusion and consideration.

She was looking at him like… He didn't know like what. He only knew it had his insides twisting into hard, painful knots. So that when he spoke, he was harsher with Saverina than he intended.

"Go upstairs."

Her eyebrows shot up, a clear sign his focus was split and he'd made a grave error. Saverina did not take well to being bossed around and he was almost always better at navigating and maneuvering her. She was the baby of the family. Spoiled in so many ways.

And the best and brightest of them. She remembered so little of the ugliness of the family, hoped for so much for her future, and had every opportunity to make a success of herself. Even without Lorenzo's help she would succeed, he knew, though he had given it and would continue to at every opportunity.

"I'll go," she said, with a raised eyebrow and

narrow-eyed look of recrimination. "*If* you come with me."

Lorenzo did not see a way out of that, so he gave a sharp nod. They would talk privately. The walk up to her room would give him time…somehow, to put his thoughts in order. To refigure a plan.

Saverina turned and Lorenzo noted she didn't look at or acknowledge Brianna. Only the boy in her arms.

"And I'll see you tomorrow, *niputi*." She leaned in and gave Gio a smacking kiss on the cheek that had the boy squealing in delight. Clearly Saverina had worked her usual magic and already won Gio over far more quickly than Lorenzo had been able to.

Still, in this moment the boy smiled shyly his way too. He hadn't called him *Dada* yet, but he no longer hid. He no longer considered Lorenzo scary.

And Lorenzo did not have time to try and continue the work he'd done there. He had to deal with his sister.

She said nothing to Brianna. Just walked past, looking over her shoulder once to nod for Lorenzo to follow. He felt all the Andersens' eyes on him. Normally he would not behave in such a way that made it look like he was some sort of servant to his sister, but…

He needed distance from Brianna. Even if he'd followed her home. Even if looking away from her was torture. Standing here staring at her in front of her parents, his sister and their son made him…too vulnerable. Too exposed.

So he followed Saverina. Away from the Andersens, to the staircase and then up toward his wing and Saverina's room.

"So. This woman," Saverina said, making no attempt to whisper or keep her voice down, so her words likely echoed and carried behind them.

"The mother of my child, you mean?" Lorenzo returned at a much more reasonable decibel level.

"Yeah. Her. What's her deal?"

"She is an artist. She is here on business. We are working out an agreement on how to co-parent Gio. Then she is going back to New Jersey." The pain carved deep, but he saw no other way.

Protecting Gio had to come first, and they could not protect him with all these swirling feelings between them, that was for certain. This he knew from experience.

Saverina stopped abruptly on the top of the stairs, whirled to face him. "With Gio?"

"Yes, but we will have a custody arrangement in place. I will not be kept from my son again, nor does she wish to keep me from him. This is all very…" He didn't dare use the word *modern* with his young sister, who viewed him as anything but. "…civilized."

Saverina made a considering noise as she continued to walk down the ornate hall to her room. She had been sixteen when he'd finally amassed enough fortune to buy this estate, so she was the only sibling who'd still been living with him permanently when he did. She'd gotten the first choice of rooms.

"So, do we hate her?" Saverina asked conversationally.

"Why would we hate her? She is the mother of my son."

"She kept your son from you."

"She had her reasons. Unfortunate though they may be, they are more Marino's fault than her own."

Saverina rolled her eyes. "You blame that guy for everything."

"Oddly enough, Saverina, *that guy* being my rival and trying to ruin my business is to blame for many of my problems."

She pushed open the door that led to her room. Even though she was off at university, he left it just as she liked so that she could always have somewhere to come home to. So that she felt like she had a home with him always.

So she would never feel alone. So she would never think the answer to any of her problems could only be solved by ending it all. *He* would solve all her problems. Always.

Lorenzo would have liked to have made his excuses now, leaving her to settle in, but he needed to find a way to neutralize the damage Saverina could likely do with Brianna.

"Why have you come, Sav?"

"Well, I called Stefano about the story I saw on the gossip site. You didn't tell me." She settled herself onto her bed, then looked up at him, still all speculation. Looking like Rocca and their mother and a grown woman when she should still be a babe in his arms.

"You should have called *me*," he returned gruffly.

"Why? To get one of your famous Lorenzo talk-arounds? No thanks." She waved an expressive hand. "We're your family, Lorenzo. I don't know when you'll get it through your thick head that it isn't just you presiding over a kingdom with us your loyal subjects."

She'd lectured him over this before, so he merely grunted and crossed his arms over his chest as response.

"So I should be nice to this woman?" Saverina demanded. "She isn't an evil witch keeping your son from you?"

"No, she is not."

"Do *you* like her?"

The question seemed innocuous enough, but nothing was innocuous when it came to his baby sister. Still, ignoring the question or giving too much of an answer would encourage her. "Yes. She is a good mother. A kind woman. A fine artist." He stopped himself from saying more because she was watching him far too closely.

"Do you love her?" Saverina asked.

Like a knife to the heart. "*Bedda Matri*, Saverina. I am tired. Go to bed," he muttered, turning for the door.

"If you can't simply say *no*, that's a yes."

Lorenzo took a deep breath. Maybe it was, but he

could only hear the pain in Brianna's voice. *I need to go home*. She needed to be away from him, and he needed to be away from her. Or they would only continue to hurt each other in ways that made no sense.

Because love was destruction. And if they didn't destroy each other, they would destroy Gio.

Just as his parents had destroyed Rocca.

"It does not matter how I feel about her, Saverina."

"Why? Is she married or something? I'm pretty sure if she was, I would have seen *that* on a gossip site."

Lorenzo stood at the door, staring at the knob. He couldn't explain it to her. She didn't understand. She didn't remember all he remembered. In her mind, their mother was a ghost. Their father a drunk, at best. Rocca... Well.

There was no doubt a sadness and a trauma there, but this was simply part of life. Saverina did not know who or what to blame the loss of Rocca on, but Lorenzo did.

"There is no *why*. We're simply being reasonable adults who are putting our son first. There is no reason to treat this as anything other than a business deal. We will come to an agreement about Gio, sign contracts if need be. Very luckily, we are on the same page about raising a child. And he will come first, always. That is what being a parent means."

Saverina was quiet for a few moments, but he heard her get off the bed and cross to him. When she spoke, it was with uncharacteristic gentleness.

"It seems to me, if you love her and agree with her

about how to raise your child, marrying her would be an option. Or at least keeping her here would be. Why would you let her go half a world away?"

Marry Brianna. He didn't let himself think of it. It didn't fit the plan. It was too dangerous. Perhaps if tonight hadn't happened, he'd be able to find some way to...make that okay.

But he'd hurt her. She'd been shaken, needing to leave and go home because *he* was too much. What they felt, far too much.

This would never make them happy. It would only tear them into pieces, leaving Gio with pieces he'd need to stitch together to survive.

Impossible.

"You can't let her take Gio back to America," Saverina said, squeezing his arm. "I know you have billions and all, but think of the sheer time commitment it'll take. Having had you as a father figure myself, I know he deserves you more in his life than that. You have to find another way, Lorenzo. One that makes *you* happy."

Happy. He wanted to laugh, but the feeling was so bitter it seemed to coat his mouth with thick ash and no sound came out. He cleared his throat.

"You do not understand, Saverina," he said very stiffly. "We have tried to make an arrangement here, but Brianna and I are too complicated."

Saverina was never so easily swayed. "You *do* love her. I can hear it in your voice. Lorenzo. You can't be so...*you* about it."

"What does that mean?"

"It means you can't plan, mold or control love so you want nothing to do with it."

It was hard to argue with that. Indeed, this was part of what made love so dangerous. He didn't see this as a bad thing. He considered it a very realistic outlook. But saying *so* to Saverina would not get him anywhere.

"So you'll just send her away? Honestly, brother, do you ever make any sense?"

He pulled his arm out of her grasp, fixed her with an icy, authoritative look. "You do not understand, Saverina. You're a child. You know nothing of caring for others. Of sacrifice."

She did not waver. She didn't so much as flinch. But any warmth in her expression turned into icy disdain. "Let's say all that is true, Lorenzo," she said very coolly. "But all that means is *you* don't know what it means to care for yourself. You don't know how to do anything *but* sacrifice. And it would be in *your* best interest if you let me show you…what all else there is."

These words were little barbs. Not quite new. Maybe she'd never expressed it quite so bluntly, but he understood this was what Saverina saw. Though he might still breathe, he was as tragic a figure as Rocca was to her.

But she didn't understand. And he didn't know how to explain it to her. Anyone.

"We appreciate the sacrifices you've made, Lorenzo. All of your siblings. Even me. But that doesn't mean we want it. You want to call me a child, and fine. To you I am. But I'm also an adult when I go off and live on my own far away from you. We all are—every one of us—adults living our own lives. We don't need your sacrifice anymore, and Gio doesn't need it at all. He needs a *father*."

Gio. He would sacrifice everything for *Gio*, but he could admit, back at the party, he'd considered his son, of course. But not in terms of *himself*. He'd thought of saving Gio the pain of watching love destroy everything.

Not that he'd have to live without Gio in arm's reach. When he'd already missed so much.

Now that he knew Gio existed, held the boy and earned his smiles, it seemed unconscionable to let Brianna return home. Saverina was right about that.

Only because he hadn't had time to think. To plan. Saverina's surprise arrival had turned upheaval even more on its head.

But this was not Saverina's fight. He did not need to discuss it with her or have her tell him what to do. That was *his* job. And he had a long night of figuring out how to deal with his large, loud family if they were all descending tomorrow.

"I am glad you are here," he said, giving his sister a look that she should read as dismissal. "While I wish you all would have waited, I am eager for everyone to spend some time with Gio. To welcome him into the family. Brianna always wanted…" He trailed off, realizing Brianna telling him about wishing she was from a larger family, *wanting* a large family was something she'd told him back *then*, not recently in regard to Gio.

Still, he could picture her face as she'd said that. She'd been trying to get him to talk about his family without directly asking him about it at a little café in Florence. She'd been wearing a red top, not unlike the red of her dress tonight. She'd say something about large families, then look at him through her lashes.

He'd known what she'd been doing, and he'd mostly kept all details to himself out of self-preservation, but every time she'd look at him, searching his face for answers, he had not been strong enough to stop some little detail from emerging.

"Brianna always wanted what?" Saverina asked, her eyes too astute for his own good.

"A larger family for Gio. It is only her and her parents. She's eager for him to be part of a larger family unit."

"Well, we've certainly got that."

"Yes."

"But I don't understand how you can let him go back to America. How you can be in love with this woman—you, Lorenzo Parisi, billionaire, and I'm quite sure a man who's never accepted a *no* in his life—and simply give up."

"It isn't giving up. It is being sensible. Gio is our focus. Anything between Brianna and me is secondary to that, and if distance is… Distance will be cleaner. More careful. It will be best. He won't end up like…"

There was a heavy silence. She should not be able to read into him saying too much, but perhaps he gave her too little credit. Perhaps no matter what he'd done to cushion Saverina, she knew that Rocca had sacrificed herself. Because their parents' warped love had broken her. Irreparably.

"Nothing you do now with Gio brings Rocca back," Saverina said gently, when she was so very rarely gentle. Because he'd taught her to be strong and demanding. He'd taught her not to take no for an answer or be steamrolled by anyone. He had tried to give her every tool he'd failed to impart to Rocca.

Saverina bringing up Rocca while looking at him with soft, wet eyes was too much. He would have stepped into the hall and slammed the door behind him, but Saverina stopped him. Never one to leave well enough alone.

"I do not know what Rocca has to do with my son," he said, looking down at her as he tried to rein his fury in.

Is it fury or hurt? Fury or love and grief?

"You can't make it so he's never hurt. People die, Lorenzo. You can't protect him from…"

"From what?" he demanded because she did not know…she could not know…

"Well, the drugs that killed our mother, for starters. The mental illness that killed our sister. You can't control people. You can only love them."

Love is a lie. Only control could protect a person from it. And part of that control was Saverina not knowing… She wasn't supposed to be that aware of what had actually happened. This was not the story he'd fed her. To save her from the truth. "I do not know what you're talking about."

"You don't think I know what happened? That our mother killed herself with drugs just as Rocca killed herself with—"

"That isn't what happened."

"Yes, it is. Rocca told me about Mom. When she was having one of her…dark periods. And I know why they both had those dark periods."

"You were a child." And no one was supposed to know. It was Rocca's secret. Even he hadn't known right away, or he would have stopped it. Stopped their mother. Berated their father into being a man and not letting his wife whore herself out to put food on the table.

Then worse, so much worse, insisting his daughter do the same.

"I was *there*," Saverina said while Lorenzo reeled. "Not so much a child as you wanted me to be. I'll admit, I didn't understand the prostitution stuff until I got older. It's only started to come together for me recently, but—"

"Stop."

"Stop what? Discussing the truth? We all know. Rocca, God rest her, did not possess the discretion about the situation that you did."

"You misunderstood her. She was…unwell and—"

"Are you calling her a liar, Lorenzo?"

It took his breath away, the accusation. The memory of his sister, so broken at the end. So desperate to stop the pain inside of her. All put there by parents who had used her.

And he hadn't been strong enough to see it. To stop it. To save her from it, or the end she'd chosen.

"How did we get on this subject?" Lorenzo demanded. This entire evening had been one moment after another where someone else was in control. Someone else was unraveling *everything*, and all without his consent. How had he arrived at this place where everyone could upend all his carefully structured walls and plans?

And still Saverina yammered *on*. As if this twenty-year-old knew more than him. Understood all while he floundered.

"I have watched you work yourself to the bone for years. And you were successful. It seemed to make you…content, if not happy. So I said very little about your choices. Oh, I know I made fun of you, but it was always a joke. This is no joke, Lorenzo. This is a son. A woman you love. And you're calling them *business*. Have you changed so much from the man who raised me so well?"

"I have not changed. I am who I have always been. My goal, my only goal, has been to protect and provide for my family. This is why you live the cushioned life you do."

"Yes. Yes, it is."

He didn't know what to say if she didn't argue with him. He didn't know what to do when it looked like she was about to cry rather than rage at him.

He was hurting every woman he cared for this evening and he didn't understand *how*. Distance. It was the only answer. Because this—discussing the past, being together, *love*—it only caused strife. Hurt.

"Without us to protect…is it all punishment for you now?" she asked, making no sense at all. "You've essentially been an empty nester for two years and I thought you might build your own life, but you haven't, have you? Rocca took her own life, so you cannot have anything for yourself?"

The words, the stark reality of them, stole his breath. Surely they couldn't be true, no matter how hard they landed. "You don't understand."

"She was my sister too. I know she was your twin, but that doesn't mean you get to own grieving her. Failing her. All that we couldn't do to save her."

He wanted none of that guilt or failure to touch Saverina. "She was my responsibility."

"She was our *sister*, Lorenzo. Not a task assigned to you by our parents. They *neglected* us, both of them. But you didn't. We weren't…bullet points on a company budget and a child isn't a business merger. I *know* you know this, so I cannot understand why you have decided to…pretend as though you are someone else."

But she didn't *understand*. Couldn't. Because he had ensured she had a life where his choices would ideally *never* make sense to her. "I am Lorenzo Parisi. I will take care of and protect my son the way I took care of and protected you and our siblings."

"You loved us too."

Love, that awful thing. Stabbing at him again and again tonight. "Why are we talking about this?"

"Because you're…messed up. Sacrificing the wrong things. And weirdly enough, when I realize I'm messing my life up, it tends to stem from some terrible thing that happened when we were kids."

The thought of her messing up, of knowing the terrible when he'd been so certain he'd shielded her from it…

"And when I realize that, and acknowledge that, deal with it—I know that's *your* influence, *frati*." She reached out to him then. Her eyes full of hurt that *he* had put there, whether he'd wanted to or not.

"*You* saved me from what could have been. Because you loved me, all of us, more than yourself. You put our needs above your own. When our father did not care, when he let everyone around him sacrifice so *he* didn't have to, you were our savior. That was…heroic, Lorenzo. You have always been my hero, no matter how I tease. But that cannot continue if on the other side of raising us, saving us, you push away any chance at love and happiness."

He was so tired of the word *love*. Saverina saying it. Him feeling it. Hating it. He pulled away from her. He was walking out the door, but that didn't stop her.

"If I was in your position, or Brianna's…what would you want for me?" she said as he walked away.

Everything good.

But not love. Because love was the root of all the bad. All the complex. All the *death*. When had love ever done anything *good* for the people in his family? It was duty, it was *sacrifice* that had saved them.

It was his mother's love for his father, and Rocca's love for both of them, that had been a curse.

But when Saverina put it *that* way, asking him to imagine her in his position, it haunted him. Because he wanted every joy for her, like he did for Gio, and he did not know how to protect either of them from all the pain that went along with it.

It didn't change his mind. Nothing would. Or so he told himself as he left Saverina and went to his office. To plan. Because feelings didn't matter. They only hurt. He would plan them away. Erect all the necessary defenses.

Saverina had said marrying Brianna should be an option, and she was right. It *would* be.

But he would put all the necessary walls in place to make certain it never broke him or her or their son.

CHAPTER FOURTEEN

BRIANNA WOKE UP feeling bruised, body and soul. She had not slept well at all. Reliving fractured moments of the art show over and over.

Not just the sex, though she couldn't lie to herself. Reliving that had her body thrumming with need all over again because she couldn't seem to put it out of her mind. The way he touched her. The way he made her feel.

What was *wrong* with her?

But she was also stuck in that moment of pain at realizing… There was no cure for what she felt for him. If she would beg him the way she had in a *public* setting, two years after he'd left her so abruptly, there was no hope for her keeping her pride. No hope to be the strong, independent woman and good mother she needed to be.

So she had to get away. She knew this on an intellectual level. Even on an emotional level, as her heart twisted over the gruff way Lorenzo had spoken to her at the show. At the arrested look on his face when he'd seen his sister.

But deep down, no matter what, she didn't *want* to go home. There was still this part of her that wanted to ignore the complications and say *yes*. Living in an estate in Sicily with her child and the father of said child was just fine, regardless of the emotional turmoil of him marrying someone else.

"You need to go home," she said aloud to herself in the hopes that saying it out loud would get rid of her doubts.

She did not know how to not want Lorenzo. Even when he made her angry, she wanted his hands on her. And she cared about him too much as a person to believe they could burn through all that lust and be left with nothing. Take away wanting him, that ridiculous heat between them, and there were still other things. There was the whole of him.

The way he looked at Gio and his sister, with a kind of pride mixed with love that made her heart swell. The way he listened—not just to her, but to her parents. Then there were the glimpses of hurt she saw underneath all that control that she wanted to soothe. Memories of *before*, when he'd listened to her prattle on about her art and made her feel special. Important.

She loved the man he was, even if she could somehow get rid of all this physical chemistry she felt for him. But they were two parts of the same coin. Something about this man—body and soul—called to her.

And he wanted to *marry* someone else, while

she was tucked away in a corner of his estate. She just…couldn't.

Could she?

She heard quiet voices and realized her mother must have entered Gio's room. She went through the adjoining door to find Mom lifting Gio out of his crib.

"Oh, you're up," Mom greeted with a smile. "I heard this one babbling and I couldn't resist."

Brianna took in Gio's sleepy eyes and the way he leaned his head on her mother's shoulder and wondered if Mom just didn't like exploring the estate without Gio as a buffer.

She smiled at her mother. Soon, Mom could be home. They could go back to the way things were. They wouldn't need to be uncomfortable in this strange world that wasn't theirs.

Except Lorenzo will be in your life, not something you can pretend doesn't exist.

She shook that gloomy thought away. "Well, we'll be heading home soon. Get back to a normal routine for you and Dad."

Helene's eyebrows drew together. "I thought you might want to…stay."

Brianna cleared her throat and expressly did not meet her mother's gaze. Instead she stared out the window in Gio's room, taking in the beautiful and expansive gardens. It would be such a treat for Gio to grow up here.

And he would. Part of the year. It would kill her to be apart from him for any swath of time, but how could she stay here? She would become pathetic in no time. She needed to be strong, like her parents had taught her to be. Never codependent.

"I think it's best if Lorenzo and I have some distance between us. I don't plan on having a custody fight, of course. Gio and Lorenzo should have a relationship and will. We'll find ways so that Lorenzo will be very involved in Gio's life."

"From half a world away?" Mom asked, not with accusation but with genuine concern.

Brianna ignored the twinge of pain and guilt. "He's a billionaire. He can fly anywhere he wants whenever he wants. He could even buy a place in New Jersey to spend some time at if he'd like. Whatever he decides, we'll come up with an acceptable custody agreement so that we each have a role in our son's life."

She sounded like him, she realized. Plans and agreements. Not the pain in her heart, or the weakness there. Maybe she should confess it all to her mother, but the idea made her feel far too vulnerable.

"You know I hesitate to tell you what to do, Bri. It's your life. Your choices. It's none of my business how you and Lorenzo decide to raise Gio."

Brianna nodded. Her parents had been lifesavers. Rocks. But they had always been very careful when it came to advice. They had been raised by difficult and overinvolved parents and had endeavored to be the opposite for Brianna.

But Brianna could *feel* her mother's disapproval. In a way she never really had before. Even when Brianna had announced she was pregnant and the father wouldn't be involved, her parents had just given her quiet support.

Never disapproval.

Until now.

Brianna turned to face her mother, determined to be strong. "But you have something to say about this decision?"

Mom took a deep breath, slowly let it out as she brushed a hand over Gio's hair. "Lorenzo is a generous man, a good father to Gio, kind to you. It's very clear you both have feelings for one another, so I'm failing to understand this insistence that you remain apart."

It felt like an unexpected betrayal. Even though her mother didn't know everything, and would likely change her mind if she did, Brianna had not expected this. She had expected what she'd always gotten from her parents. Unconditional support.

"The problem is…complicated. Lorenzo and I are complicated."

"Life is complicated. I think it's very clear he has feelings for you, Bri. The way he looks at you. *Anyone* can see it."

"A look doesn't mean much, Mother."

"Maybe not, but don't you owe it to Gio to try? To stay here and see what you and Lorenzo might be able to build. As a family. Lorenzo clearly has a very good idea of what family means. Saverina was telling us about all the brothers and sisters he raised. He's a good man, Brianna."

"I'm very well aware."

"Then why would you go home? Why put Gio through custody arrangements? Why put yourself through that? I want to support you, Bri. I always want to support you, but I'm just lost here. Help me understand."

Understand. What was there to understand? She supposed last night was the best example of why she couldn't stay. He couldn't fathom marrying *her*. He didn't understand...anything.

Then shouldn't you want to stay and teach him?

But how did you protect yourself and teach a brick wall?

"He wants to marry someone else," Brianna said, turning back to the window and staring at one of the trees outside sway in the wind. "He took a *date* to that art show." She tried not to let that hurt throb in her voice. "He... I know he has feelings for me. I do *know* that, but he doesn't believe in love. He thinks it's a lie. A fairy tale. I don't know why, when he has so much love to give, but I have not been able to get through to him, and I have made some bad decisions in the process. It's best for me and Gio if there's more...separation. If I'm not throwing myself against a brick wall." Did sex count as throwing herself against a brick wall? It sure felt like it.

"So you told him you love him?" Mom asked.

Brianna thought back to every interaction. She chewed on her bottom lip. "Not in so many words, but he knows."

Helene pressed her lips together. More uncharacteristic disapproval. "Perhaps you should tell him."

"You don't understand."

"No, I'm sure I don't. And I don't need to. Your relationship gets to be your own, but you've always been a very...self-contained type of person."

Brianna looked at her mother, surprised this was the corner more hurt was coming from. "What does that mean?"

"It's not a criticism, Bri. It's just... I could see where there might be some room for confusion. Have you told him, bluntly, how you feel? What you want?"

Brianna felt a somewhat hysterical laugh bubble up inside of her. Didn't sex at a party say enough? "He knows," she repeated. She had told him she wanted a relationship built on love. Wasn't that clear enough?

"Are you *sure*?"

Brianna was sure. *Almost* sure anyway. Maybe she hadn't told him she wanted *him* to be the loving relationship, but why would he tell her love was a lie if he didn't know she loved him?

Unless... Unless he was worried about *his* love for her, not hers for him. Unless all of his thoughts and fears when it came to love had very little to do with *her* love...and everything to do with his.

Maybe...maybe if he knew, maybe if she assured him that she loved him, it might help him get over his reticence.

Don't be an idiot, Brianna.

"Men are not always the most adept at understanding emotions and feelings," Mom continued. "Sometimes you think you've been very clear, but they're still in the dark. The things I've had to explain to your father over the years." She rolled her eyes. "Lorenzo is quite adept in many areas, but perhaps he needs some help and some more directness in interpersonal relationships."

It sounded so…rational. So correct. She *knew* she was letting herself get her hopes up when she shouldn't, but this was her mother. Helene Andersen was a model of clear thinking and good decision-making. Shouldn't that mean Brianna should listen to her? She turned from the window and looked at her mother.

It made her feel so vulnerable it hurt. To believe any of this could be true. But her mother held Gio and looked so…in control. Like she knew what she was doing.

"Do you… Do you really think so?" Brianna managed to ask.

Helene took a long moment to answer. "Bri. I can't promise you that he will behave in the way you might want. I can't promise you his feelings. But I can promise you it's better to try than not. It's not…quite the same. Family love. Romantic love. But when I made the decision to cut things off with my family, it was because I knew I had tried *every* avenue. Any pain I feel over that loss is…grief, not guilt. Because *I* gave it my all. At the end of the day, you can't control Lorenzo, make him think or feel what you want, but it's better to give it your all and fail and grieve that, than spend your life wondering and feel guilt or regret."

Brianna wasn't sure she believed that. Wondering left...avenues. Mental gymnastics. Baring everything could be the definitive end, and wouldn't that hurt worse than the possibility?

But her mother was looking at her expectantly, holding a little boy who looked so much like his father, who *deserved* a father—*his* father in his life. Maybe... Maybe she was too scared to do it for herself, but she should do it for Gio. For Lorenzo.

"I guess... I guess I should go talk to him."

Mom smiled broadly and Brianna used that as courage. She went back to her room and got dressed and practiced what she would say.

Lorenzo, I know you think love is a lie, but I love you. I have since the beginning. I think we should try to make something work. Can't you at least try?

Well, that made her want to throw up. It sounded so much like...begging. And she wouldn't beg. She had to have *some* pride, didn't she?

Does pride matter to your son?

Someday it would. Someday he would be old enough to look at his parents and understand the complicated world around them. Brianna wanted Gio to grow up thinking she was a good person, a good example. She wanted Gio to feel the same way about her that she felt about her parents.

Could she be that if she kept throwing herself at his father...and failing?

She looked at herself in the mirror. She couldn't hide the effects of her lack of sleep. She couldn't hide anything if she was going to go tell him she *loved him* and wanted a chance. She would be the pathetic character in the situation if he kicked her to the curb. The sad little girl begging for crumbs where there were none to be had.

But she…she *did* believe he loved her. Or cared for her at least. He wouldn't behave the way he did if he didn't have *some* feelings for her. Was it really so pathetic to be up-front and honest with him and demand the same?

No, it didn't have to be pathetic. Not if she kept her wits about her.

And when have you done that when it came to Lorenzo?

Wasn't there some saying about insanity being behaving the same way over and over again and expecting different results?

But if she could get through to him… Wasn't it possible that she got through his walls, his plans, his *love is a lie*, and get to the heart of the matter? Even if it wasn't love on his part, if they could be honest with one another, maybe that was the actual answer. Maybe that would take away their inability to resist a physical relationship.

She moved out into the hallway because spending any more time getting ready was just going to continue her roundabout thoughts. She needed to take action. Decisive action.

She shouldn't get her hopes up. With her luck

she'd end up saying nothing and having sex with him in a closet or something. Then he'd tell her he had a plane ready for her to return to New Jersey.

She huffed out a bitter little laugh. Why was she doing this?

But as she stepped into his office, she knew *why*.

She loved him.

Lorenzo was holding a young girl who didn't look any older than Gio and speaking to a man who could have been his twin. He had a broad smile on his face. This was the man she'd fallen in love with. This was the man she wanted.

But when he noticed her there, everything changed. Stiffened. But he acknowledged her, bidding her forward.

"Brianna, this is my brother Stefano."

Stefano held out a hand and she shook it. His smile was wide and easy. "My wife had to take the baby up for a diaper change, but she's eager to meet you and Gio."

"We're eager to meet you all as well," Brianna managed with a smile. It wasn't a lie. She wanted Gio to have all this. To look around and see people who looked like him, who shared his blood, who loved him because they were connected by bonds that could only be broken if you chose to break them. Aunts, uncles, cousins. She wanted it *all* for her son.

"Well, I'll apologize in advance. You get us all together and it can be overwhelming, but I can assure you my wife and I have done a lot of work to train everyone not to inundate the children with attention if they aren't having it." He took the girl from Lorenzo as if to demonstrate. "Which is why this one needs a little nap before the rest of the troops arrive. I'll be back down for the eleven o'clock conference call, Lorenzo."

Lorenzo nodded and said nothing as Stefano took the shy little girl out of the room. And closed the door behind him.

Which was for the best. This was a very private conversation and it looked like privacy might be on the premium once the rest of the family arrived. But Stefano had also mentioned a conference call. It *was* a workday, she supposed. She just wasn't sure how much that mattered to a billionaire. "Do you have a few moments to talk?"

Lorenzo pointed to a chair in front of this desk. "Yes, I was actually going to request your presence once I was done with Stefano."

He spoke very carefully, but he didn't look like himself. He looked…tired. Like perhaps he too had struggled to sleep. Had he thought of what they'd said?

Or what they'd done?

Brianna tried to think of neither, but the dark room at the party loomed large in her head. She had begged him last night. *Begged.* Her cheeks had to be red as tomatoes at this point because it all replayed in her head like an erotic movie.

But he did not smile charmingly. He did not point it out. He stood there. Stiffly. Businessman Lorenzo Parisi, nothing else.

"I have come up with an alternative plan to you returning to New Jersey," he said, clasping his hands behind his back and moving to stand behind his desk. Like they were in a business meeting. Or she was an employee and he was about to fire her.

She was here, trying to spell her feelings out for him—for the first time—and he was…planning. Plotting. Controlling. She wanted to roll her eyes, but she tried to hold on to some patience. He didn't know what she wanted to say.

"I think we should talk before you offer any… plans." Like he just got to make the plan and she'd jump to it.

He shook his head. "No. I've made the plans. This is what we'll do."

The man could be such a tyrant. "Lorenzo, my God." She was about to get up, whirl away, march off, pack a bag and *never* look back.

Except he's the father of your child and you don't get to just run away like he did before.

She took a deep, settling breath and focused on what she'd come here to say. "I want to discuss—"

"We will marry."

She thought maybe she blacked out for a minute and hallucinated those words. Just yesterday he had talked about marrying someone else. Just last night he'd been on the same page about her going home. "Excuse me?"

"As much as I would like to grant you your space, after calming down and giving it some thought, I realized I simply cannot live with Gio so far away.

I have missed too much already. I know you won't leave him, nor should you. He should have both mother and father within reach at all times."

"What does this have to do with getting *married*?" Brianna asked, pinching the inside of her arm to make certain she wasn't having some kind of bizarre fever dream.

But he stood behind his desk, looking remote and determined, even with the exhaustion evident on his gorgeous face. "You did not care for the idea of me marrying someone else, so *we* will marry. We will find a way to very carefully divide our lives, but we will both live on this property so we both might be in our son's life."

It was what she wanted. Sort of. But she thought of last night. Even if he didn't marry someone else, they weren't on the same page. The only thing they agreed on was Gio. And she could live like that, but not on his property. Not *married*.

"We will be married in name only," he said, fully driving that point home. "We will live separate lives on the same piece of property. We will not engage in relationships with anyone else, so there will be no jealousy. We will not be alone with one another so there will be no…temptation. Your parents and my siblings will act as buffers."

It wasn't that it sounded so terrible, it was just that she didn't understand where this was coming from. She didn't understand how he thought he could just make pronouncements like that. "And we have to marry for this ridiculous plan?"

"I will need to be married at some point in the next few years for optics' sake. If it bothers you that it might be someone else, it might as well be you."

It might as well be you.

Ouch.

Brianna scrubbed her hands over her face, trying to make some sense of this man. Some sense of her feelings for him when he was clearly...delusional. At best.

"How can you stand there with a straight face and say we will be separate, have no relationships, and there will be no jealousy?"

"Because it is what I've decided. Because it is the best course of action."

"Great. We're *people*, Lorenzo. People grow, change, *feel*. They don't always choose the best course of action, as we've demonstrated the past week. Because making the right choice always is... hard. Because *always* choosing the best course of action is a little bit soulless."

He waved a hand, as if dismissing it all. "People should make a conscious effort to be better than all that."

For a moment she simply sat in the chair and stared up at him. He was serious. He truly believed all it took was an *effort*. As if last night could have been avoided if they had better *effort*.

She got to her feet, needing to do something or she might simply explode. So she began to pace. "I cannot fathom why I am so desperately in love with you when you are the densest man alive." That wasn't exactly how she'd meant to tell him, to say the words. He had to know, but this was the directness her mother had spoken of.

"Love is a—"

"Yes, you think it's a lie. A fairy tale. I get it." She waved a hand in a broad gesture as she turned and paced toward him. "Well, no, I don't. Because you love your son, and so quickly. You love your sister, your brother, your niece and so obviously that it's there on your face when you're in the same room with them. I suppose you had some bad experience with romantic love. Funny enough, so did I. I wish you leaving me the way you did had cured me of the fantasy of it all like your experience did, but alas."

He stood there, very still, but there was something in his eyes. That flash of pain. Whatever it was he kept well hidden and buried. Whatever it was that made love a lie in his mind.

She had never asked, she realized. Her mother had urged her to be direct and Brianna hadn't been cognizant of just how indirect she'd been. She had tried to know him before, but it had not been direct questions. It had been careful, roundabout conversations.

Little had changed since he'd been back in her life. The one direct question she'd asked him, about why he'd broken up with her, had gone unanswered. She'd let it.

Now she realized that she needed to know what he held back. And that meant she had to be brave enough to ask rather than live in fear. Fear of how he'd react to her poking her nose in it. Of what it might be. Of how it might hurt *her*.

Was this love if she didn't have the courage or strength to ask? To continue asking until she got true answers?

"You will stay," he said, again. His plans, always the answer. "We will marry. We can wait a year or two if you'd rather, but we *will* marry. And we will keep our distance. I do not believe introducing the idea of 'love' into our marriage will do anything except hurt Gio."

She crossed to him, trying to be brave enough and sure enough to face down whatever this was. She put her hands on his chest and looked up at him. "*Why* do you think that?"

He looked down at her, icy and remote. But underneath that was *something*. If only she had the strength, the determination to reach it. So far they both had been very good at running away from those sore spots.

Something had to change. She looked up at him, at that cool, remote facade he worked so hard at. She had to be the one brave enough to challenge him. To work on herself to get through to him.

If she wanted *more*, if she wanted *love*, she couldn't change *him*. But she could try to deal with *herself* in order to get through to him.

"Tell me, Lorenzo. What hurt you? What made it so impossible for you to believe in love when it comes to *me*. Because I know you love Gio. I know you love your sister. Your brother. Your niece. It's evident in everything you do, every second you're with them. And I know…" For a moment, her voice faltered, but she thought of their son. Everything he deserved. A father who worked through his demons was one of them. A mother strong enough to face down uncomfortable truths was another. "I know you care for me in *some* way. So what is the lie?"

She expected *something* from him, and she supposed that was her first mistake. Thinking she could get past whatever walls he'd built.

"This is not open for discussion, Brianna. I have made the plan. We will marry. We will lead separate lives. That's final." He stepped away from her. Like she was *dismissed*.

She wanted to keep being strong. She wanted to believe her mother was right and she just hadn't found the words. But this was almost as demoralizing as last night. It didn't matter if he loved her if he refused to acknowledge it. She couldn't *change* him, she knew this.

So why was she trying?

"You won't bend, even a little? Even for your son?"

"Everything I do is for my son."

"Well, me too, Lorenzo. So my answer is no. No. I won't do it."

He scowled at her. "I do not understand how you could refuse me. This will solve all our problems."

"No, it won't. You can't seem to grasp *my* problem. It isn't that I love you. I don't mind loving you. Maybe if I thought you didn't love me back, that would be more uncomfortable. I don't know. But it's impossible because you do love me."

"Love, love, love!" he muttered. "Why is this all anyone speaks of?"

"Because it's important? It makes life meaningful? You love so many. Why do you refuse to accept that you love me? What is so wrong with who I am? What I am?"

For a moment, there was something in his expression. A softness and a pain that she thought meant she'd gotten through to him. But he didn't speak.

He also didn't leave.

So she pressed on no matter how much it hurt. Because she loved him. She wanted him to accept that love as much for herself as she did for him. She could make him happy. They could *be* a happy family if he'd just let her in. "I don't understand what you're afraid of. But I understand you're afraid. Tell me—"

"I am not afraid of anything. Every challenge in my life I have met head-on and will continue to do so. You have no choice in this matter, Brianna. I am in charge."

In charge? No, she didn't think so. She'd had enough. "Why?"

For a moment, his mouth opened and no sound at all came out. Like he couldn't *fathom* the question, let alone an answer to it. "What…do you mean?"

"What exactly are you threatening me with to keep me in line, to assert you're in charge? Because you aren't the president of me. Or the CEO. You can't just make decrees and expect me to follow them.

We're just two random people in the world. So why are you in charge? How are you going to assert this? Are you going to fire me? Well, I'm not your employee. Are you threatening me for custody? I don't think you are. Maybe you want to kill me off? That would be the simplest way."

His jaw clenched. "Brianna." So disapprovingly.

"You're so used to everyone jumping to do your bidding, but I cannot go against my best interests. I *love* you. I will do a lot of things to put Gio first. I would sacrifice almost anything for him. But I can't sacrifice myself—every happiness. If I did, he would feel it."

"He will have us both. Every privilege and opportunity afforded to him. He will have family. That is what matters."

"Those things *do* matter. But so do I. And so do you. Being parents doesn't mean we have to be robots, sacrificing every emotion for our child. We get to be human." Maybe it wasn't romantic love that had made him bitter. His parents were dead, so she hadn't given much thought to them, but maybe they were responsible for what he thought of love. "What did your parents do that hurt you so much? Perhaps I should ask your sister. Maybe she'd be more forthcoming."

That certainly got through to him, but he didn't warn her off. Didn't divulge any family secrets. He just stood there, looking like a sailor lost at sea in a storm. She wished she could reach out and be his anchor.

But he'd have to choose it first.

"You may ask Saverina whatever you wish. You may find out every dirty family secret. Be my guest, Brianna," he said, so coldly she shivered. "But I will not change my mind, and if you wish that to be a threat, so be it."

Then he stormed out of the office, leaving her no better than she'd been when she entered. Just more hurt.

But she had tried. Her mother was right. If she had left without trying, there would have been guilt. She would have had regrets.

Now she could return to New Jersey free of all that.

If only she could be free of loving him and hurting for him.

CHAPTER FIFTEEN

LORENZO SAT AT the long dining room table surrounded by his family. His *entire* family. Somehow they had managed to all come this weekend despite the fact that every Christmas was a circus act trying to get everyone home at the same time.

Suspicious.

But nothing was more suspicious than Brianna interacting with his siblings. Smiling and laughing along with them, like she hadn't come to his office earlier and dropped all sorts of bombs.

Like she was *enjoying* herself.

And why shouldn't she be? He'd taken care of everything, hadn't he? He'd spent his afternoon neutralizing another round of stories about Brianna and Gio planted by Dante. He'd moved forward with his plans to renovate the north end of the estate to outfit Brianna and her parents and build an art studio.

She remained safe and taken care of because of *him*. She would not enjoy the same back in New Jersey.

She should be thanking him. She should be following all his plans to the letter with nothing but gratitude. Because that would be best. For *everyone*. He always did what was best for everyone. Because if he didn't…

Brianna wasn't Rocca. He'd never let her be put in a position where she had to sacrifice so much.

Rocca should be here.

It was his failure she wasn't.

But he hadn't failed again. He was surrounded by evidence of all he'd done. The way every step from that mistake, that loss, had been exactly the right one.

He looked around the table. So many voices. Laughter, little arguments, children's meltdowns. It was the sound of a job well done. There weren't loud, angry fights. No one here had to worry about money. No one had to sell themselves for a scrap of bread. No one here had to lose themselves in a haze of drugs in order to deal with the weight of the things they'd done to survive, to earn a dollop of praise.

Because *Lorenzo* had stepped in. Unlike their useless father. *He* would have let them starve. *He* would have let them all be ruined.

Lorenzo refused.

So he should be able to enjoy it, his success, but he couldn't, because Brianna sat shoulder to shoulder with Saverina and Isa, Stefano's wife, discussing *something*. Meanwhile, Gio had voluntarily climbed into Lorenzo's lap and was playing a kind of peekaboo game with Karl, Valentine's partner, the two of them the last to arrive, coming all the way from Germany.

Why had Saverina done this to him? The whole evening was interminable. And he struggled to stick with any conversation because his gaze kept traveling to Brianna. Thinking over what she'd said in his office. What she'd said last night.

Watching the way she fit right in. Her and Gio, even her parents. They didn't feel like a little American island, out of place in the midst of his loud, opinionated family.

It all fit.

And Brianna loved him.

He had known she cared for him. He had been afraid she loved him—well, no. Not afraid. That wasn't the right word. *Concerned.* But her saying the words this morning… It shouldn't change anything. The words weren't a surprise.

So why did he feel rocked to his core?

"I love you. I will do a lot of things to put Gio first. I would sacrifice almost anything for him. But I can't sacrifice myself—every happiness. If I did, he would feel it."

Those words haunted him. On a constant loop.

If I did, he would feel it.

As if sacrifice, as if control and plans would *hurt* Gio, when everything he was putting in place was to protect Gio. Just as he'd done for all his siblings over the years he'd finally been in control.

Brianna came over to him, and she didn't meet his gaze. She looked at their son.

"I better put this one to B-E-D," Brianna said, holding her arms out to Gio. The boy went easily, but he smiled at Lorenzo as he did. He was warming up. Step by step. And Lorenzo knew that time would only strengthen their bond. Gio would never remember Lorenzo had missed out on him as an infant.

Gio would only know his constant presence. Because it *would* be constant. No matter what Brianna said *no* to.

"Say good night to Dada," Brianna said to Gio.

"Night, Da."

It was the first time Gio had actually said *Da*. The boy clearly didn't feel the weight of that first, but Lorenzo did. And when he lifted his gaze to Brianna, he knew she did as well. It would be a moment that would stick in his memory for all time.

Gio in his mother's arms. Lorenzo's family chattering around them. And one simple word. *Da*.

Brianna turned away quickly, Gio in her arms, her parents trailing after her. Leaving him to face down his family. The exit of the Americans seeming to put everyone's attention squarely on *him*.

"Saverina says you're in love with her," Valentine offered, rather loudly, considering the Andersens had only *just* left the room.

Lorenzo skewered him with a look.

"I heard that she loves him right back," Stefano offered.

"Then why is she still planning to leave?" Saverina demanded. "What is *wrong* with you?"

"As lovely as this little family reunion is, without the excuse of Christmas, I can't imagine why I'd put up with it." He tried to get up, but Accursia, who sat on his other side, put her hand over his.

"Because we're your family and we care about you, Lorenzo."

"You're desperately in love with her," Isa said, holding her dozing baby in one arm and the glass of wine she sipped from in the other hand. "It's obvious to anyone with eyes."

He had missed that baby stage with Gio. It hurt, even knowing he would never let Gio out of his life again. That year without the boy would always hurt.

Because that was what love did. Crawled into all your weak spots and *hurt*. It worked when it was your family, people in your care, because you could stop all that hurt with sacrifice. With careful planning and important walls for distance.

"I am never desperate, I assure you. Everyone speaks of love as if it is some great thing, but the only thing love does is destroy. That is all *I* have ever seen. A good marriage is not based on *love*, it is based on mutual understanding."

"Are you insinuating my husband doesn't love me?" his sister-in-law asked, with such an open, innocent expression on her face only experience told him she was needling him.

He spared her a quelling glance, but she was clearly unmoved. He moved his gaze to Stefano, but Stefano had put an arm around Isa and looked as disapproving as his wife did.

"This is *my* life," Lorenzo reminded his family.

"But you're mucking it up," Saverina insisted with

a certainty Lorenzo could only chalk up to youth and a lack of experience. She continued on as if *she* knew all. "And every time we've just about mucked up our own lives, you've stepped in to correct course. So, guess what? We're all stepping in to correct *your* course."

"It's kind of comforting," Valentine said, studying the wine in his glass. "That you *can* need correction. You aren't *so* perfect."

Lorenzo scowled even deeper at his brother. "All right. If I am not perfect, and you are all so old and wise now, what should I do?"

"I know what you shouldn't do," Stefano offered. "Demand a loveless marriage. Declare plans like a general giving orders to a soldier."

Isa and Saverina's eyes widened as they stared at him. "Is that what he did?"

Stefano nodded as Lorenzo fumed. "How do you know anything of what I've done?"

Stefano shrugged, wholly unconcerned. "I eavesdropped."

This time Lorenzo did stand, pulling his hand out from Accursia's. "You have crossed a line, brother." To think all that Brianna had said might have been listened to. That they might all know…

"Yes. I wonder where I might have learned to do that."

Lorenzo shook his head. "I have raised all of you. Protected you. Afforded you every opportunity. And this is how you repay me? Come here without warning, criticize my every choice, eavesdrop and gang up on me? Very well. Clearly I have failed."

"Oh, don't be such a martyr," Saverina said. Then, when he glared at her, she rolled her eyes and even faked a yawn.

He made a move for the exit, but Saverina stepped in front of it. Valentine blocked the other exit.

"No running away today because you didn't get to control the situation," Stefano said. As if he had any right. "Time to face up to some very important facts."

"We're all grown up," Saverina said, working in tandem with Stefano from the opposite end of the room. "It doesn't mean we might never need you, but not the way we once did. Now you're free. Do you really want to spend that freedom like some kind of robot monk when you have a nice, smart woman with a backbone, far as I can see, who shares a son with you and *loves* you?"

"None of you remember what love does?" He looked at Stefano and Valentine, because though he'd tried to shelter them, they were the closest in age and likely knew as much as he did. Then there was Saverina, who'd known more than he wanted her to. Maybe they all did.

But Stefano and Valentine were standing there, both with partners. Stefano with children. A family. Love.

How could they bear it?

"I don't blame *love* for what happened to Mother, Lorenzo," Stefano said, all of his nonchalant defiance gone. In its place was a calm if sad reverence. "Real love does not demand sacrifice. Real love is not what we witnessed—the desperate need to please someone else."

Lorenzo watched as Isa put her free hand on Stefano's arm. A simple, silent comfort. "Some relationships are toxic, Lorenzo," she said, with something warm in her eyes that felt too much like pity. "Some people make choices because they aren't mature enough to handle their consequences, or because they were traumatized and haven't dealt with it, or any number of other reasons. From everything Stefano told me—"

"You told her?"

"She is my wife. I've told her everything about our childhood. It is how I work through those traumas."

"Have you told Brianna anything of Mother? Of Rocca?" Saverina asked gently.

"Why would I?"

"So she could understand. So you could deal with it. You can put us all in our little boxes. You can put your memories in some sort of lockbox under eighteen kilometers of denial, but it's still *there*. And no amount of planning or control changes the past."

"That is why we focus on the future."

"Yes," Stefano agreed. "But *your* future. Not plotting out Brianna's or Gio's, but actually thinking about what *you* want."

"I am a *billionaire*. Everyone in my care is well taken care of. What more could I want?"

"That's a question only you can answer," Stefano said. Very quietly.

But it echoed like thunder inside of Lorenzo. Especially as everyone began to get up. His siblings walked by, brushed kisses across his cheek, patted him on the back, but they all filed out and left him alone. The last thing said: *That's a question only you can answer.*

He wasn't sure how long he stood in the dining room. Alone. When he finally convinced himself to leave, he knew he should go to his office. Check on the moves Dante was making. Get to work on the renovations, the studio building—because Brianna wasn't leaving. He refused to let her.

So why are you in charge? How are you going to assert this?

He didn't know yet, but he'd find a way.

Still, when he walked by his office he didn't stop. He walked out the back of the house and into the gardens. He hadn't known she'd be here.

Had he?

But she was sitting on a little bench he'd had installed that he sometimes sat on when he needed air and solitude. The trees weren't in bloom this time of year and it was too chilly for her to be out here.

But somehow he'd known she would need air after all that, just as he did.

She must have heard him, because she turned. He watched her as she straightened her shoulders, lifted her chin. As she braced herself for dealing with him.

Why had he come? He knew he would not get

through to her yet. He had no plan. No threats or entreaties. Only this black, roiling thing inside of him that threatened to have him begging at her feet.

Because that was the kind of behavior love brought out in a person. Desperation. Pathetic, destructive needs. Hers or his, it did not matter.

"Your family is lovely."

"That is not the word I would use in this moment."

Her mouth curved ever so slightly. Then she sighed. "Well, I'm very tired. I should get to bed." She stood, but he stopped her.

He wanted to ask her what he should want. He wanted her to lead him. It was unacceptable, but he couldn't let her arm go. He could only stand here, blocking her exit, holding on to her. Her soft, chilled skin under his fingers. He couldn't resist drawing his hand up her arm, pulling her closer.

She even went, without censure or resistance. Until he'd pulled her to his chest. Where she belonged.

She looked at him. He'd expected a flash of anger or something, but all he saw was a grim kind of exhaustion. "We can do this again, Lorenzo. God knows we'll enjoy it." Tears shone in her eyes. "But it won't change anything. Is that what you want?"

Why was everyone suddenly so concerned with what he wanted? "You want to know what I want?" He dropped her arm and staggered away from her, everything inside of him threatening to erupt. He strode away, then back and pointed at her. "I want you to listen to reason. To do as I say."

"To think as you think? To feel as you feel?" she returned, again sounding more tired than frustrated.

He was frustrated. "Yes!"

"I wish I could. It would make things so easy, wouldn't it? If I could be your little lap dog, but I am not."

Lap dog. It brought up all those unpleasant memories. What his mother had twisted herself into. All for love. Because his father had never been moved. By his mother's pleas. By her sacrifices. He'd never thanked her. He'd only found more blame.

That was love.

"You think you understand, but you do not. You should trust me on this. I only seek to do what is right for all of us. You cannot defy me on this. I cannot let you."

"Why did you come out here, Lorenzo? To say the same things? To have sex again?" She shook her head, but she didn't move away. "Something has to give. If it cannot be you, if you cannot love me, if you cannot give me a *chance* for something real, then it will be me. Leaving. It is the only way *I* know how to sustain this. I love you, but—"

"You think… You think you love me. That I love you. You think this can lead somewhere, but I know what love does."

She looked up at him, those tears swimming in her eyes. The same from this morning. The same entreaty. She even reached out and clutched him. And he had his sisters' and brothers' words ringing in his ears. About love and trauma and responsibility. About wants. About life—lives they'd all gone out and built…while he'd built an empire. For them.

"Lorenzo, tell me. Tell me what you think love does."

"It breaks everything!" It was a shout, tinged with all the pain and then it was as if some dam broke. The dam he'd built up himself, with every piece of responsibility, control and grim determination.

Now it was in pieces and the words rushed out. "My mother loved my father. She was desperate to please him. She would have done anything for him, and it never mattered. You cannot love away destruction. You will get there eventually, or I will, and the hurt we will cause in our wake will be…catastrophic. If you or I give in to it, we will destroy everything."

"What did your mother do, Lorenzo?"

He stood there, breath coming in short pants, but somehow Brianna maneuvered him back to the bench, into a sitting position. She even slid next to him, taking his hand into hers and settling it on her lap while her other arm came around his shoulders.

"Tell me, Lorenzo. Tell me everything."

He shouldn't. Knew there was no point, no outcome that changed the things he'd seen, the things he'd survived. But the dam was gone, and so the story poured out. "We were very poor. I don't remember anything else. Every time another child came along, food on the table got more scarce. Arguments about work, money. My father couldn't keep a job. He could never stand anyone telling him what to do."

Brianna nodded, sitting there next to him. Warmth on a cool night as her hand rubbed up and down his arm.

"I'm not sure when it started. She didn't want to do it. I know she didn't. But my mother would have done anything to make my father happy. Yes, to put food on the table for us, but she could have demanded *he* do something. She wouldn't though. He was her world, and she wanted to serve him. She loved him so much. I can't count the times I heard her crying over how much she loved this worthless man. She didn't want to, and he shouldn't have let her."

"What did she do?" Brianna asked gently.

"She got a job where she worked at night. I believed this for a very long time. That she was off being a waitress somewhere. That it was all on the up-and-up. Even as she…became less and less herself. But I suppose we all believed it because we wanted to. Because it brought money in. We were scraping by. Rocca and I acted as parents. Father drank. Mother became more…erratic. Then she got pregnant with Saverina and had to stop working her mysterious night job."

Lorenzo knew he should stop there. It was enough. Surely she understood now, but the words continued. "Father said Rocca could take Mother's place at her job until Mother was back on her feet. Rocca was only fourteen. I insisted I should do it, but Father said it was only women's work. So I kept my job at the butcher shop during the day. Watched the children at night. Rocca helped with the children at day and worked at night. While my mother loved our father and he did *nothing*."

"You must be so proud, Lorenzo," Brianna said. "So many sacrifices, and those children you raised are in your home. Responsible adults. Good people. Who love you."

"Not Rocca." Was that his voice? So ragged. So weak? But these were words he'd never spoken. A story he'd never stitched together for anyone but himself. And it was something about that, about Rocca's memory, that seemed to insist he finish it.

"She was my twin sister. We were more parents to everyone than our own, but... She began to act like Mother. More erratic. Depressive episodes. Mother went back to work and I suggested Rocca not work there anymore, but Father insisted. Still... I didn't know."

"What didn't you know?"

He sucked in a breath. It shook all the way out. "They were prostitutes."

Brianna's grip on him tightened, but she said nothing. Only held him there. As though he weren't to be blamed for all this. She didn't speak. Not to argue, not to offer platitudes. Not to be so shocked and horrified he felt the need to hide it all away again.

She simply sat there. Holding his hand. Waiting. As if... As if, as Isa and Stefano said, talking about these secrets, these horrors could help a person *work through them*. Understand them.

And it was that dinner tonight, and this woman

here, who finally dragged the words out of him. Just by being here. Just by loving.

"I began to find out things…later. A client introduced Mother to drugs at some point, and the… price for her went down. Eventually it was the drugs. She died of an accidental overdose, but I still did not know. I should have. Rocca continued on. She never told me a thing. But like Mother, she became more erratic. I told her she needed to quit this job. I would scrape together more money. I would find a way to get her another that didn't affect her so. At first, she refused, but then… After Father died, it was as if something lifted and she finally explained everything to me."

"Poor girl," Brianna murmured.

"I was so stupid. So blind. I should have seen it. I got her out of there once I understood. I tried to get her help, but she was…"

Everything in him felt ragged. He was a million jagged edges. Pain. So much pain. Because Rocca should still be here. If he'd known, if he'd had a chance to step in, she would.

Brianna stroked his hair. "Their sacrifices weren't your fault, Lorenzo. You were a boy."

"I should have said something. Stood up for her. For them both. If I was only a boy, Rocca was only a girl." Because how could he absolve himself when they had been a team? And only one of them had suffered so?

But it was as if Brianna did not see this as his weight to bear alone. Because she didn't leave him.

She didn't accuse him. She just kept speaking and holding on to him.

"Here is one thing I know about you, and I think all of your family knows too. You would have. If you'd known, if you'd had the opportunity, you would have sacrificed everything for them. Your father is to blame here. *He* knew. If she told you after *he* died, he had some hold over her."

It had never occurred to Lorenzo. Maybe he'd never let it occur to him. Blame felt so much more controllable. So much stronger.

But Brianna was right, and he could no longer deny that as much as he wished he had known, could have done something, the adult in the situation had made it impossible.

"Just because you couldn't sacrifice instead of Rocca doesn't mean… My love, this is a terrible story full of tragedy, but you have done everything you could in the shadow of that tragedy. Sacrificed for your siblings. Gave them everything."

"Not Rocca."

"No. But that is on your father. You took on the role of adult because the adults would not. But why does it mean we can't love each other? We aren't your parents. Our love does not need to be like your mother's. For one, we both love each other. And you are so clearly nothing like your father."

"But I hurt you. At the party. When I brought Natalia. When I suggested I marry someone else. In that room, you cried and said you had to go home. That is my fault. That is what love does. It hurts."

"Yes," she agreed. So easily.

He looked at her because she made no sense.

"I'm still standing, Lorenzo," she said, calmly. Accepting every word as a truth when… When it wasn't. "People hurt each other. It's that whole human condition you seem to think you can escape. By making yourself everyone's…boss, father, ruler, whatever. But you can't be any of those things to me, so you have to keep me away?"

"You don't understand."

"No. I'll never understand what you went through. I won't ever pretend to. But I love you regardless. I don't need to understand to love you."

"I will ruin you. The way my father ruined my mother. If you'd just… If we make a plan, if we stay apart, if we treat it like business, we can make it okay." He knew how desperate he sounded. How afraid. All those things he'd convinced himself he wasn't. But those feelings were there in his voice. In his heart.

She shook her head. "No, Lorenzo. I can't do that. I wasn't there. I didn't know your parents. I don't know what either of them went through, what they were thinking when they did the things they did. Maybe I'd do the same thing in their position, but I am not in their position. Neither are you. We have the power to make our own choices. Some of them will be mistakes. But loving you, even when it hurt, even when you walked away, has never been a mistake. It has given us Gio."

Gio. The boy he'd only known a handful of days,

who already owned his heart. That Parisi face with blue eyes. A shyness that warmed into love so easily. His heart. His soul. Just as this woman who'd listened to all he'd said and…loved him through it. Saw him in the middle of all that hurt.

She had not walked away. She had not laid blame. She still spoke of love as if… As if his mother's behavior was her own choice, her own feelings. As if his father's indifference and blame weren't stamped into Lorenzo's bones.

As if the hurt he'd caused her was the "human condition," to be dealt with and forgiven. Not a poison that would ruin them all.

"I know you would give Gio everything," Brianna continued. "Just as you've given your siblings everything. You are not your father and never have been. You have always put the people you love first. But it must be a balance, Lorenzo. You must give yourself the space to also have *your* wants and needs met. Giving yourself over to your sacrifices and your business doesn't make you any different than your mother if you do not take care of yourself along with it."

This hurt. *The human condition.* But again, Brianna did not leave. She did not drop the accusation and withdraw. She loved him through it.

Stefano had told him only he could decide what he wanted. And it wasn't that he didn't know. Of course he wanted Brianna. And not just because it would keep Gio close, but because she had always been the sunshine in his dark. Ever since he'd first laid eyes on her.

But he was so *afraid*. Not concerned, no. Terrified. Of what love had done to his mother. Of the utter destruction wrought, not just on his parents, but on Rocca.

Destruction. That had come from two damaged people. A love that had blotted out responsibility and the love his mother should have had for her children. Because there had been none of the balance Brianna spoke of. Only a kind of selfishness.

One neither he nor Brianna possessed. No matter how scared he was, he believed Brianna. Standing here in his garden, pouring her light into him.

"I've never been poor," she continued. "So I won't trivialize how important money can be, but our son deserves a father who isn't afraid of love. Couldn't you at least try to give him that?"

It was a million moments coalescing. Hurtful ones and healing ones. Saverina's voice asking him, *"If I was in your position, or Brianna's...what would you want for me?"*

The same as he wanted for Gio. For Brianna. For everyone...

That's a question only you can answer.

What did he want out of this life? The courage to give his son everything. Brianna had said that she could not sacrifice her happiness because Gio would be touched by that. She was right. Giving Gio *everything* meant also...allowing himself balance. Love. Light.

"I fell in love with you the moment I saw you, Brianna. More every moment we spent together. Nothing has ever terrified me more."

She reached out, cupped his cheek with her chilled hand. "You dazzled me. And underneath all that dazzle was a man I could not help but love. It never went away, Lorenzo. Even when I wanted it to. This doesn't have to destroy us."

"But what if—"

"We can't what-if ourselves out of this. There are too many. Those first days as a mother, my entire head was what-ifs. So many things could have gone wrong, but my mother gave me advice I have held on to ever since. Any person can only do their best with what they are given, and that best is cushioned by love."

Lorenzo didn't want it to make sense. Didn't want to believe it was enough, but why... Why was he so bound and determined to make things harder on himself?

Rocca took her own life, so you cannot have anything for yourself?

Saverina had said that to him, and he had spent the past day trying to deny it. Desperate to ignore it. But it was true. His entire life since he'd lost his sister had been punishment. Because he'd loved her, but he hadn't been able to save her.

If he looked back with an adult's maturity and experience on everything that had happened when he'd barely been an adult, he knew Brianna was right. He had done all he could.

It hurt, but it was true. Love had not been enough, but that didn't mean it was poison. Still… "I could not stand to lose you."

Her thumb brushed back and forth across his cheek. "Loss is inevitable. But I'd rather lose knowing I'd held everything I loved close, than that I'd pushed it away and never enjoyed it."

He had already missed time with Gio. Missed these two years with Brianna. If he had not, perhaps he could not have accepted her words. But the past two years had taught him that if he could dig under his fear, holding on was better than hiding.

"I love you, Brianna. I want to do that perfectly, so that you never hurt."

"I wish that were possible. But loving is enough, Lorenzo. I promise you. We can love each other *and* ourselves. Love our son so brightly that even those hurts will be cushioned by all we've given him. I'll show you. If you'll let me."

He covered her hand with his. He held her gaze. And he made a promise to her, and to himself. "I will. We will marry and—"

She shook her head, even though she didn't pull her hand from his grasp or lean away from him. "I can't marry you, Lorenzo."

Confusion swept through him. "But—"

"Not yet. But I'll stay. And we will work through…everything. Our pasts. Our hurts. Your trauma. We will build a foundation. And once the foundation is strong, we'll discuss marriage again."

Lorenzo did not argue. Perhaps she was right. Perhaps building and foundations and *working through* were the things missing when love failed so spectacularly. He would not fail at this. Not now. For Gio. For Brianna, and also, strangest of all, for himself.

Because as his siblings had tried to get through his head earlier, as Brianna had stated this morning when she'd confessed her love to him, he deserved some of his own wants as well.

"You will at least share my bedroom, Brianna."

She laughed. A bright, beautiful laugh like sunshine. She would always be his sun. She leaned into him, and they wrapped their arms around each other. "Naturally."

She made it seem like love could be an answer instead of a fear. A hope instead of destruction. Maybe he was a fool to believe in it, but how could he not believe in her?

He would believe in her, and he would prove to her that he could do love as well as anyone. He would not be afraid. Not anymore.

And they would be married within the year. End of story.

EPILOGUE

THE WEDDING WAS one for the ages. With a family the size of Lorenzo's it was hard not to be. Brianna and Lorenzo had agreed to let the press be involved in the reception, but the ceremony was to be all theirs.

Dante had tried over the course of the past year to plant more stories besmirching Lorenzo's reputation, but the more Lorenzo didn't care, the more it did not matter. The press got tired of trying to paint him the villain when all he ever seemed to do was work, dote on his wife and son, and refuse to ever retaliate against Dante.

Sometimes living well really was the best revenge.

And they had lived well. They had learned each other all over again. They had let their families mesh and meld and they had worked to parent Gio together. It had not always been easy, they did not always see eye to eye, but when Gio had turned two with a party full to the brim with aunts, uncles, cousins and his grandparents—just as Brianna had always wished for—Brianna had realized it was time to make things official.

Since Lorenzo proposed almost every week since that night when he'd finally confessed himself to her, she only had to wait two days, then finally surprise him with a yes.

He'd gone into wedding planning mode immediately.

Well, not *immediately*.

Now here she was in an ancient church, while Saverina and Accursia and her mother fussed over her. Right before she was to join her father and walk down the aisle, Saverina pulled her aside.

"I was wondering if you would put this on your bouquet." She held a tiny picture frame on a pin in the palm of her hand. In the frame was the picture of a teenage girl, smiling, looking so much like Lorenzo Brianna immediately knew who it was.

She blinked desperately so as not to cry and ruin her makeup. She gave Saverina a nod and Saverina attached it to the ribbon around her bouquet. They hugged, both doing their best to keep the tears at bay.

Then it was time.

She stood, her mother on one arm and her father on the other, as the doors opened. Gio stood at the end of the aisle next to his father, wearing a matching suit.

"Mama!" he called out, doing an excited little dance that had the entire church laughing, including Brianna. She walked down the aisle, and her father and mother handed her over to Lorenzo. Gio wrapped his arms around her leg before being gently coaxed by Stefano and Valentine to stand next to Lorenzo.

Brianna looked up at Lorenzo with a bright smile. His gaze swept over her, stopping once at the little picture frame in her bouquet. He took a deep, steadying breath, then lifted her hand to his mouth.

He brushed a kiss across her knuckles, reminding her of a night long ago in Florence. That had changed the entire course of her life. And had given her everything she could have ever dreamed of.

So when they said their vows, she had no doubts. Love was not the enemy.

It was the answer. Always.

* * * * *

If A Son Hidden from the Sicilian
swept you off your feet,
then why not try these other stories
by Lorraine Hall?

The Prince's Royal Wedding Demand
Hired for His Royal Revenge
Pregnant at the Palace Altar

Available now!

COMING NEXT MONTH FROM

Ⓗ HARLEQUIN
PRESENTS

#4137 NINE MONTHS TO SAVE THEIR MARRIAGE
by Annie West

After his business-deal wife leaves, Jack is intent on getting their on-paper union back on track. He just never imagined their reunion would be *scorching*. Or that their red-hot Caribbean nights would leave Bess *pregnant*! Is this their chance to finally find happiness?

#4138 PREGNANT WITH HER ROYAL BOSS'S BABY
Three Ruthless Kings
by Jackie Ashenden

King Augustine may rule a kingdom, but loyal assistant Freddie runs his calendar. There's no task she can't handle. Except perhaps having to tell her boss she's going to need some time off...because in six months she'll be having *his* heir!

#4139 THE SPANIARD'S LAST-MINUTE WIFE
Innocent Stolen Brides
by Caitlin Crews

Sneaking into ruthless Spaniard Lionel's wedding ceremony, Geraldine arrives just in time to see him being jilted. But Lionel is still in need of a convenient wife...and innocent Geraldine suddenly finds *herself* being led to the altar!

#4140 A VIRGIN FOR THE DESERT KING
The Royal Desert Legacy
by Maisey Yates

After years spent as a political prisoner, Sheikh Riyaz has been released. Now it's Brianna's job to prepare him for his long-arranged royal wedding. But the forbidden attraction flaming between them tempts her to cast duty—and her *innocence*!—to the desert winds...

#4141 REDEEMED BY MY FORBIDDEN HOUSEKEEPER
by Heidi Rice
Recovering from a near-deadly accident, playboy Renzo retreated to his Côte d'Azur estate. Nothing breaks through his solitude. Until the arrival of his new yet strangely familiar housekeeper, Jessie, stirs dormant desires...

#4142 HIS JET-SET NIGHTS WITH THE INNOCENT
by Pippa Roscoe
When archaeologist Evelyn needs his help saving her professional reputation, Mateo reluctantly agrees. Only the billionaire hadn't bargained on a quest around the world... From Spain to Shanghai, each city holds a different adventure. Yet one thing is constant: their intoxicating attraction!

#4143 HOW THE ITALIAN CLAIMED HER
by Jennifer Hayward
To save his failing fashion house, CEO Cristiano needs the face of the brand, Jensen, to clean up her headline-hitting reputation. But while she's lying low at his Lake Como estate, he's caught between his company...and his desire for the scandalous supermodel!

#4144 AN HEIR FOR THE VENGEFUL BILLIONAIRE
by Rosie Maxwell
Memories of his passion-fueled night with Carrie consume tycoon Damon. Until he discovers the ugly past that connects them and pledges to erase every memory of her. Then she storms into his office...and announces she's carrying his child!

Get 3 FREE REWARDS!

We'll send you 2 FREE Books plus a FREE Mystery Gift.

Both the **Harlequin® Desire** and **Harlequin Presents®** series feature compelling novels filled with passion, sensuality and intriguing scandals.

YES! Please send me 2 FREE novels from the Harlequin Desire or Harlequin Presents series and my FREE gift (gift is worth about $10 retail). After receiving them, if I don't wish to receive any more books, I can return the shipping statement marked "cancel." If I don't cancel, I will receive 6 brand-new Harlequin Presents Larger-Print books every month and be billed just $6.30 each in the U.S. or $6.49 each in Canada, a savings of at least 10% off the cover price, or 3 Harlequin Desire books (2-in-1 story editions) every month and be billed just $7.83 each in the U.S. or $8.43 each in Canada, a savings of at least 12% off the cover price. It's quite a bargain! Shipping and handling is just 50¢ per book in the U.S. and $1.25 per book in Canada.* I understand that accepting the 2 free books and gift places me under no obligation to buy anything. I can always return a shipment and cancel at any time by calling the number below. The free books and gift are mine to keep no matter what I decide.

Choose one: ☐ **Harlequin Desire**
(225/326 BPA GRNA)

☐ **Harlequin Presents Larger-Print**
(176/376 BPA GRNA)

☐ **Or Try Both!**
(225/326 & 176/376 BPA GRQP)

Name (please print)

Address   Apt. #

City   State/Province   Zip/Postal Code

Email: Please check this box ☐ if you would like to receive newsletters and promotional emails from Harlequin Enterprises ULC and its affiliates. You can unsubscribe anytime.

Mail to the Harlequin Reader Service:
IN U.S.A.: P.O. Box 1341, Buffalo, NY 14240-8531
IN CANADA: P.O. Box 603, Fort Erie, Ontario L2A 5X3

Want to try 2 free books from another series? Call 1-800-873-8635 or visit www.ReaderService.com.

HARLEQUIN
PLUS

Try the best multimedia subscription service for romance readers like you!

Read, Watch and Play.

Experience the easiest way to get the romance content you crave.

Start your **FREE TRIAL** at
<u>www.harlequinplus.com/freetrial</u>.